Shore Leave

Anastasia McKellan

CHANCES PRESS

www.chancespress.com

Shore Leave

Chapter One

Greg Marsters climbed out of the beat-up pick-up and hauled his duffel bag over his shoulder. He drew in a deep breath of salty sea air and looked out over the rows of boats glistening in the morning sun in the harbor. Then he looked up at the small, shabby town nestled in the hillside above.

Wyndham Shores, Massachusetts hadn't changed in decades, and he wondered if it ever would. No surprise it looked exactly the same way it had the day he'd left eighteen months ago. The Navy had sent him to San Diego for six months, and he'd spent the year before that on a boat off the coast of Africa. He'd longed to spend his two weeks of leave somewhere familiar, and this place was the closest thing he had to home.

His folks had moved away years ago, but Greg still had the house he'd bought when he and Maxine married. She hadn't fought him for it in the divorce, and the house gave him somewhere to go when he had leave to burn.

Emmett Culligan had hired him to help with his boat restoration business, and in two weeks Greg would finally have enough money to buy the boat he'd had his eye on in Shoreman's Harbor. The Navy didn't pay him enough to buy such a luxury unless he saved up. He'd stashed every penny he could.

He made his way down the dock. Most of the slips in the marina were still full, but the summer tourists would be out soon, paying a small fee to have one of the guys take them sailing for the day. He walked past Old Timer and Wyndham's Joy, tour boats that had been around since he'd been a kid.

"Hey, old friends. Ready for an adventure today?"

The boats bobbed up and down in the water in answer, and Greg smiled.

Emmett had always tried to keep them in good shape, but they looked a little worse for wear. But hell, who didn't in this town?

The bullet wound in his side ached while he walked, like it always did in humid weather. He put a hand over it. The doctors told him it had healed up nicely, but the pain flared ever now and then. Phantom pain was all he could figure.

Thunder rumbled overhead and Greg patted the duffel bag. He'd packed an extra pair of jeans and T-shirt, a thermos, and a sandwich. No umbrella. Then again, what was a little water on his clothes?

He made his way down the dock to Lady Lucky, the forty-eight-foot wooden schooner that would consume his next few weeks. Emmett was already hard at work laying in a piece of new hardwood on the deck, and he squinted up at Greg.

"You're late, fly boy."

The lines creasing the old guy's grizzled face had deepened, and his dull light brown hair looked shaggier than the last time Greg had seen him. Too many years in the sun had taken their toll.

Greg knew for a fact he'd gotten to the docks five minutes early, but didn't dare challenge Emmett by glancing at his watch. "It won't happen again."

"Get out of bed on time from now on. Being a Navy pilot and all, you should be used to getting up before the crack of dawn, right?"

"Yes, sir."

Emmett shook a gnarled finger at him. "Don't smart mouth me. I won't take any lip from you."

"No, sir. You won't get any." Greg shook his head. He hadn't been smart mouthing, but he'd learned years ago that arguing with Emmett never got him anywhere.

Emmett's eyes narrowed. "Good. You'd do well to keep yourself in line."

Greg nodded. That was the plan. Towing the line for the next couple of weeks. He'd help renovate Lady Luck and save his money and get the hell out of town the second he could.

"What are you waiting for?" Emmett nodded to the duffel bag. "Put your stuff below deck. We've got a lot of work to do. We'll get this hardwood laid in, then polish her till she shines."

"All new hardwood, huh?"

"All new."

Greg looked at the boards on the dock. The handcrafted dark wood gleamed, and he knew Emmett had put his soul into making it. "Looks good."

"We've got a lot to do and not enough time to do it."

"I'm ready."

Greg had almost forgotten what putting up with Emmett day after day was like. But he'd handled it before and he could handle it again.

Greg dropped his bag below deck and squinted in the glary light as he came back up. Someone approached the dock. From the look of it, a woman with long brown hair, wearing cut-off shorts, a T-shirt, and sandals.

"We expecting company?" Greg asked.

"Melanie Grantham," Emmett said. "You know her, don't you?"

"We went to school together."

They'd been in the same kindergarten class and classes here and there up through high school. He'd had gym with her one semester, and he'd seen her at football games or in the lunchroom with the group of girls she'd run around with. He and Melanie had never been close, but she'd always been around.

"I don't get around as well as I used to and she's helping me keep my books," Emmett said. "She helps out on the boat. At the house. Wherever I need her."

Greg watched Melanie walk down the dock. It might be nice to have someone to talk to besides Emmett the next few weeks.

"Has she been in Wyndham Shores all this time?" Greg asked.

"Hasn't left. Why?"

Greg shrugged. "Just asking."

He watched her as she came closer. At five-foot-three or so, she had a slender build. The cutoffs revealed a pair of pale legs; not particularly long, but smooth and supple. The V-neck of her pink T-shirt showed off the curves of her cleavage. Her breasts were small but proportioned to her body, and Greg's mouth suddenly went dry picturing her naked. Where the hell had that come from?

"Don't get any ideas," Emmett squinted at Greg like he'd read his mind. "You stay away from her and from all the other women around here. She's got work to do and so do you."

"Yeah. Will do," Greg muttered.

He hated to admit Emmett was right about anything, but the older guy had a point. Greg needed to stay away from women. He'd gotten himself into enough trouble and he'd do well to be on his own for a while.

Sometimes the loneliness got to him, though. He felt it the most when he got off a plane and the guys had wives and families waiting for them on the tarmac, while he headed off alone. And he felt it when his single friends opted to spend time with their girlfriends rather than go for a beer. Not that he faulted them for a second, but love felt like a lost cause for him.

His ex-wife and everyone in this town loathed him and wanted him to live the life of a monk as punishment for what he'd done. He'd lived that life for eighteen months. It had been tough but he'd do it for as long as he needed.

Melanie stepped aboard Lady Luck, and Greg found himself the focus of her attention as she gave him a wide smile, her eyes sparkling. "Morning."

Greg nodded.

"Mornin', Mel," Emmett said.

She held up a white plastic bag. "I brought breakfast, only I didn't know there'd be three of us—"

"Greg's going to be working for me for a few weeks."

Melanie gave a quick glance at Greg through her dark lashes. "Haven't seen you in a long time."

"No, I—"

"He's helping fix up Lady Luck," Emmett said in a gruff voice. "And that's all he's going to do around here."

Ignoring Emmett's comments, she smiled and reached a hand out. Greg took it.

"That's good." Melanie's smile widened. "We can use all the help we can get."

Her hand felt soft and smooth, but he released it and drank in the sight of her.

"Mel, can you get him on the payroll—"

She nodded. "I'll have the paperwork ready this afternoon."

She smiled, and Greg liked the sweetness of it. He hadn't seen many smiles lately and she had a beautiful mouth. She had a heart-shaped face with porcelain skin, and he'd always thought she was pretty in a girl-next-door kind of way. She'd pulled her long, wavy dark hair up into a ponytail, making her look about eighteen when he knew she had to be ten years older than that.

Melanie set the bag with breakfast down. "I'll leave the breakfasts for you both."

"You take one for yourself." Emmett nodded at Greg. "Flyboy here's on his own."

"I, uh…already ate," Greg said.

She blinked, as if it wouldn't be polite to have brought only enough for Emmett and herself. "It's no trouble to pick up another breakfast—"

"You eat it, Mel," Emmett said.

Melanie gave in and nodded. "Emmett, I've got some checks for you to sign. I'll take them to the mailbox later today. That should take care of your bills for the month."

"Go on and sign those checks for me." Emmett wrapped up a rope on deck. "I trust you."

Melanie nodded.

"I'm starving. Gonna eat," Emmett said.

"I'll get started laying in that wood," Greg offered.

"You can start starboard side. I'll be back to check your progress."

Greg nodded, then watched Emmett as he grabbed what had to be a breakfast sandwich wrapped in wax paper out of the bag. The old guy went below deck.

"He likes to eat in private these days." A mischievous smile came over Melanie's face. "It's the only relaxing he does all day. He also doesn't like anyone to know he does the crossword puzzle in the morning paper, but I've caught him a couple of times."

Greg laughed out loud, the sound echoing around the dock. His reaction surprised him. When had he last laughed?

"Did he always do crosswords?" Melanie asked.

"Never. He worked around the clock. He wouldn't be caught dead doing a crossword puzzle."

"Ah, then it's something new."

Melanie's eyes twinkled, maybe pleased that she'd made him laugh. Her eyes were a unique shade of blue, the color of a dark blue sky, surrounded by thick lashes a shade darker than her dark brown hair. He sensed a depth in her eyes, and a sadness, like much had happened to her over the years. Not all good things. Still, she looked fresh and un-jaded compared to most everyone else in this washed-up town.

"Do you want coffee?" Melanie asked. "He's got a pot down there."

Greg shook his head. "I'll have water later." He nodded toward her food. "You should eat."

She sat on one of Lady Luck's benches and opened the bag of food. "If I didn't know better I'd think Emmett had it out for you."

"Yeah. Well, he's not alone."

He figured he didn't have to explain to Melanie. Everyone in town knew about what Greg had done to Maxine, and they knew about what happened afterward. Or thought they knew. Nobody had given him a chance to tell his side of the story.

"I guess people haven't been that friendly to you," she said.

Not after what he'd done to the town's Golden Girl and the other woman he'd wronged in the process.

"They didn't exactly break out the welcome wagon," he said. "But then again, I wouldn't expect them to."

He'd made a huge mistake, and that one stupid mistake had cost him his wife and his friends. Everyone that meant anything to him had turned their back on him, and he'd had to start his life over. Wasn't that punishment enough for his crime?

Greg took a look at the planks and eyed the deck. He knew exactly where to place them.

"You've worked for Emmett before, haven't you?" Melanie asked.

"Yeah. Back in high school. A couple of summers in between then and now. He's taught me a lot over the years."

"People say Emmett's the best at what he does."

"Yeah, he might be a little rough around the edges, but he's a master renovator."

"He said he's already got a couple of people interested in Lady Luck," Melanie said.

"I have a feeling he might keep her for himself," Greg said.

"Not so sure about that. I have a feeling he'll use the money to buy two more boats to fix up. He wouldn't know what else to do with himself."

Greg smoothed his hands over a piece of wood.

"You should eat something before you start working," Melanie said.

"I'm okay."

"Here." She tore her egg sandwich in two and tried to hand him half. "Better eat it quick before he comes up and sees."

Greg shook his head. "You eat it. I'm not hungry."

"I'll bet you haven't eaten anything this morning."

"I'll be all right."

Melanie took a bite of the sandwich. "Emmett didn't mention you were going to start working for him today."

"Probably something he'd rather forget." He nodded to the sandwich. "Maybe I'll have some of that sandwich after all."

She handed him half and smiled.

"Thanks." He chewed fast.

He snuck a glance at Melanie while they ate. She'd crossed her legs and he caught a glimpse of supple, muscled thighs. He couldn't tear his gaze away. He wondered what it would feel like to have those legs wrapped around him, then chided himself. He didn't come here for sex and he'd leave Melanie alone.

***

Melanie chewed her breakfast sandwich. Of all the guys who could have come to town…she would have at least liked the chance to look decent this morning. Emmett liked throwing her surprises every now and then, and Greg on deck was definitely a surprise. She would have taken more time with her hair and put on some makeup. Maybe worn a little dress or something instead of a pair of old cutoffs.

"You know, you're the first person who's been nice to me since I got back," he said.

"There are two sides to every story," she replied. "I know that no one's let you tell yours."

"Ah, nobody wants to hear my side."

"I do."

She'd thought today would be exactly like every day had been for the past couple of months, but Greg showing up would definitely break up her summer. She'd been nose to the grindstone, saving every dollar Emmett paid her so she could afford to finish up classes in the fall at the local community college.

Between taking care of Emmett's accounting, booking sailing tours for tourists, and helping out at the harbor and at his house, she'd had little time to socialize. Although Greg didn't look like much of a talker. As she recalled, he'd always preferred work over chatting.

Greg looked better than ever. His green T-shirt complemented the rich green of his eyes, a thick arm muscles flexed beneath the shirt whenever he moved.

She'd always wondered what those big arms would feel like wrapped around her.

She'd always loved his face: the hard line of his jaw, the dimple in his chin, and the way thick stubble began to grow in at the end of the day. She even loved the tiny scar on his cheek. Many times she'd imagined running her fingers through the thick crop of dark brown hair, feeling the silky texture on her fingers. By the end of each summer it always turned a shade lighter from him being out in the sun.

Despite everyone else's opinions, Melanie had always thought Greg was a man who knew how to treat a woman. After her horrendous marriage ended six years ago, Melanie would have welcomed the chance to date a guy like him. She'd dated the past few years, but she always moved too fast and expected too much, and then got disappointed when it turned out the guy didn't feel the same way about her. She might be a fool, but she still hadn't completely given up on the idea of finding someone who loved her as much as she loved him.

"Emmett's lucky to have you," she said.

"I'm lucky to have the work."

Melanie's friend Amelia was the only person in the world who knew about her secret crush on Greg. Amelia empathized, but they both knew nothing would ever happen between them.

Greg had come from a respected military family. His father had been an admiral in the Navy and everyone knew Greg wanted to follow in his footsteps. Everyone in town had looked at Melanie and her father as trailer trash, and Greg had never looked twice at her.

Every guy in school had been attracted to Maxine, and Greg had been no exception. With her long, silky black hair and model-like face, Maxine had been the envy of every girl in high school. Her whole family had been the envy of everyone in Wyndham Shores. Her father had been the Chief of Police and her family had been the richest in town, with a huge, sprawling house and nice cars. Maxine had always worn brand name jeans and tops, with different shoes and jewelry to match every outfit. She'd set the trend for everyone in their class. Her dramatic makeup had always been perfect, accenting her soft brown eyes and perfect, full lips.

Melanie had been lucky to have had a couple of pairs of jeans and some hand-me-down sweaters. She'd flipped burgers at the local hamburger stand, waiting on all of her classmates who came in, and could only envy what Maxine had.

Greg had always been way out of Melanie's league, and she couldn't expect him to be interested in her now.

"So how long are you here?" Melanie asked.

Greg nodded. "Two weeks."

She grinned. "You look well. The Navy agrees with you."

"It's a good job. An adventure."

"I always thought you were the adventurous type." She smiled. "So you're planning on sticking with it."

"Oh, yeah. No question."

"Good." She finished the last bite of her sandwich and brushed her hands together. "I guess you've gotten to travel all over the world."

He nodded. "I've seen a lot."

"Do you like that?"

He nodded.

"I've always wanted to see the world," she said.

He stopped sanding and looked at her. "Why can't you?"

She drew in a breath. She barely had money to cover bills and basic necessities. "Easier said than done."

"Yeah. Guess it is."

"I'd like to travel one day, though."

He gave a slow nod, and she could almost see the thoughts swirling in his eyes. He looked world weary. Like life had taken its toll on him. She saw it on his face. He had to be thirty by now but he had a maturity in his eyes, and any passing stranger would think he was older than that.

Emmett came back up the steps. "You two ready to work?"

"Ready," Greg said.

Greg winked at Melanie, unsmiling, but she beamed inside at their little shared moment. How would she get through the next few weeks with Greg at her side? She had a huge crush on him and didn't want him to know. How foolish would she feel if he ever found out how she felt about him?

No, it would have to be her little secret. One she planned to keep forever.

Chapter Two

By late afternoon Greg had gotten soaked in the rain. After it stopped, he went below deck to shower and change into dry clothes so that he could finish the rest of the day's work. He laid in the last piece of hardwood for the day and knelt to clean up the supply cabinet.

"I've got some paperwork for you to sign."

He almost bonked his head on the cabinet at the sound of the familiar feminine voice. Melanie had surprised him.

She held out a clipboard and smiled. "So Emmett can pay you."

Greg nodded and took the clipboard from her. He looked up at her while he signed. He'd missed her. He hadn't liked it when she'd left the docks to run errands. Emmett's craggy face and his scowls had begun to get to him already, and he'd longed for her friendly face.

Greg signed the documents. "It's nice having you around."

Melanie's blue eyes brightened. "Yeah?"

"Yeah. I thought I'd be stuck here with Emmett the entire day."

"It's nice having you around, too. Emmett can be a little overbearing, but his heart is in the right place. You know that, right?"

"Yeah, I know that," Greg said. "I watched him with you today. He keeps an eye on you. Makes sure you're taken care of."

Melanie's smile widened. "I'm like his surrogate daughter, now that Erin's gone off to college."

"I know he cares about you, but he runs you ragged."

Melanie shrugged. "I'm used to it."

Greg still didn't like it.

Melanie locked up the paperwork and they headed off the boat. It was six o'clock. Still plenty of daylight. His stomach rumbled and if he didn't get food soon he'd pass out. But he didn't have even a scrap of food back at the house, much less beers in the fridge. He'd been lazy about grocery shopping and wouldn't be able to put off heading to the store much longer. But his stomach ached at the thought of eating yet another meal alone.

He didn't want trouble, but he needed food and he wanted company. Female company would be even better. The thought of going home tonight to his dark, empty house didn't appeal. It depressed him being there alone these days.

"Can I buy you some dinner?" Greg asked while they walked up the dock.

She blinked and stopped in her tracks. "Oh."

"Sorry." He slapped his forehead. How stupid could he get? And how much of an idiot did he have to be to think they could eat dinner together? He backed up, wishing he could take his request back. So much for staying away from everyone around here. That had lasted what, all of thirty seconds?

He'd grab takeout from the diner and go home and eat in front of the TV, and fall asleep on the couch. Before he knew it, it would be time to come back to the harbor.

"You probably have to go home to your family," he said. "Sorry."

She shook her head. "I live alone."

"Come on. You're living with some guy who'd strangle me if he saw me walking with you."

Melanie smiled and shook her head. "No. I'm with anyone. Not even dating at the moment. You're the one I should be worried about—"

He lowered his head.

"No, I just meant...I'm sure you're dating some-one who'd miss your company this evening," she said.

For a second he'd thought she'd been referring to his infidelity. But he realized she hadn't been, and that relieved him. Something made him trust her, like she wasn't out to jab him or out to get him every chance she got like everyone else. He could use a friend right now.

"I'm not dating anyone," he said. "In fact, I, uh…I couldn't be more single."

Melanie gave him a mischievous look. "No woman waiting for you at your house, wondering when you'll come home to her?"

He shook his head. "No one. Between you and me, there hasn't been anyone since Maxine."

"You're serious."

"I've been staying out of trouble."

He didn't know why he wanted Melanie to know there hadn't been anyone else, but he felt the need to be honest with her. He got the feeling she was honest with everyone and deserved the same thing in return.

Her voice brightened. "Okay, then. Since we're both single, dinner would be nice."

"Great."

"How about the diner at the end of the dock?"

"You don't want something fancier?"

She shook her head. "The diner's fine. I like the food there."

"The diner it is, then."

The few couples they passed stared at them as they walked up the dock. The diner may not have been the best choice to have a private dinner, Greg thought, but he couldn't think of anywhere they could go in town where everyone wouldn't know him. Everyone knew everyone in this town.

He knew for a fact that two of his fellow officers had come home to Wyndham Shores over the past few weeks and the town had thrown a party for them on a Saturday night. Dinner. Music. Dancing. Guys he'd gone to school with. Twelve years ago by now. But Maxine and her family had made sure no one would ever open their arms to Greg again. And the second he and Melanie walked in the diner, he knew that no one around here would ever be throwing him a party.

Most of the small tables along the wall overlooking the marina were full. As they found a booth off to the side, two couples and a group of four women in their sixties and seventies stopped eating and turned around to look at them. The older women whispered amongst themselves, and two of them shot Greg dirty looks.

Greg gritted his teeth. "You're taking a big risk talking to me."

Melanie settled into the booth. "Why?"

He slid in across from her. "I'm not exactly anybody's favorite guy around here these days."

She grabbed menus from the side of the table and handed him one, eyes meeting his. "People around here have strong opinions. Sometimes they don't wait to hear the whole story and listen to the facts before making judgments."

He opened the menu. "What about you? Do you think you know the facts?"

"No, I don't. Which is why I'll withhold judgment," she said.

"You must have some idea of what happened with Maxine and me. Some opinion of what happened."

"I've heard all the rumors. All I know is you don't trash a man the way people have done with you."

"Maybe I deserve the trashing."

She gave him a sad smile. "Of all of the men I know, Greg, you're the last one to deserve being trashed," she said softly.

"You don't know me that well."

She closed her menu. "Do you remember that day in high school? You must have been about sixteen."

"What day?"

"Eric Robertson decided to beat up on Kevin Potter. And you wouldn't have any of it. You tore Eric away, and he ended up splitting your lip."

Greg laughed. "Thanks for the reminder." He touched his mouth. "It's healed up now."

"I know, but…what I'm trying to say is, I would never think the worst of a guy who'd done something like that."

Nice of her to say that, but…

"I think you're alone in that opinion," he said.

"Too bad. I'm not changing it."

Greg closed his menu.

"What are you having?" she asked.

"Breakfast for dinner. Flapjacks, bacon, eggs, and toast."

"Good choice."

"What about you?" he asked.

"Same thing I always get. An open-faced turkey sandwich with mashed potatoes and vegetables."

"That's your favorite, huh?"

She smiled. "I like Thanksgiving all year round."

Their server, Eunice, had worked at the diner since the dawn of time. She stopped in front of their table and opened her pad of paper. "Having your usual, Mel?"

Mel nodded. "Thanks, Eunice."

Eunice scribbled down their orders and left.

"You come here a lot then," Greg said.

"At least once a week."

Greg nodded. "You work hard. Does Emmett get a lot of tourists taking his boats out?"

Melanie nodded. "Tourist season is crazy. We're busy. Emmett needs a lot of help. One person can't run this place alone."

"He pays you okay, right?"

She nodded. "More than I can make serving food or in the gift shops."

Was that the only thing she thought she could do? "You could do more than serve food and work in a gift shop."

She smiled. "How do you know?"

"I saw the way you worked today. You keep Emmett going. He wouldn't know what to do without you. You're running his life and you're invaluable. You could take those skills anywhere and work for anyone you wanted. Hell, you could run your own business if you wanted."

She bit her lip. "Maybe. Easier said than done, though."

"I guess that goes for everything."

She cleared her throat. "I'll tell you what I'm saving for. But you can't laugh."

"No, I won't."

"I'm trying to finish my associate's degree in nursing."

"Really?"

She nodded. "I couldn't get into a bachelor's program. My grades aren't all that great, and I didn't have the money. But if I can get my A.D.N. I'll have a better shot."

"Sounds ambitious of you. How much longer do you have in school?"

"If I pass all of my classes this summer and fall, I should finish in December." She shrugged. "It's going to be a long road."

"Good for you for having goals."

"And what about you? Do you plan to have your own ship one day?"

He grinned. "If I said I did, would you laugh?"

She gave him a serious look. "I'd never laugh at your dreams."

He looked down at the table, not sure what to think of this woman in front of him. Was she serious? After being with someone who criticized his every move, he didn't think there was any such thing as a woman who'd support him. He didn't think he'd ever have that, but Mel was easy to talk to. Then again, she wasn't depending on him the way Maxine had been, so he couldn't disappoint her. There was no risk on Melanie's part.

Melanie had the sweetest face and she gave him the sweetest smile. He couldn't believe he'd never paid much attention to that smile. Right now it warmed him from the outside in. Her lips looked soft and supple and he wondered what it would be like to taste them with his.

When their food arrived, she dove into her plate. Greg watched her eat for a second.

She stopped and looked up at him with a sheepish expression. "Sorry. I haven't eaten since breakfast. And I have a big appetite."

"You don't look like it," he said. "You look like you eat like a bird."

"Sometimes I do eat like a bird, and then I'm starving by the end of the day."

"That's not good, Mel—"

She glanced up at him. "I got too busy today to eat."

"Does that happen a lot?"

She nodded. "Sometimes. There's so much stuff to do I just don't have time."

"You should eat if you're hungry. To hell with Emmett's work."

"Easier said than done sometimes."

"Yeah, I know. But you have a beautiful body. You should treat it well," he said.

She looked taken aback, and he swore he saw her cheeks pink up. Hadn't anyone ever said that to her before?

"Even if you didn't have a beautiful body, you need to take care of yourself."

She picked at her food with her fork for a second and stared down at her plate. "I suppose you always take good care of yourself?"

"I always eat, no matter what."

She looked up at him with sparkling eyes and laughed. "That's good."

The group of ladies had finished dinner and walked past them toward the front door. Greg caught a look of death from one of them. It stung, and he frowned. Why did he have such a hard time shrugging off nasty looks from strangers?

"Is it bugging you being here with me?" he asked Mel.

"What do you mean?"

"Is it making you uncomfortable?" He shifted his weight. "Everyone keeps staring."

"Let them stare. I'm glad I'm here with you."

"I guess they're curious."

Melanie nodded. "Maxine was back in town visiting her folks and maybe they think you'll run into each other."

His stomach dropped. "Will we?"

Melanie shook her head. "She went back to Georgia."

"With her new husband?"

Melanie nodded. Then she bit her lip. "Sorry. I didn't mean to bring up a—"

"No, it's fine. I'm glad you brought up her moving away with Allen." His gaze met hers. "I was so stupid. I made such a fool of myself trying to get her back after what happened. Talking about her new husband makes it all real, that it's over and we're over. A done deal. I should have realized it a long time ago. She wants nothing to do with me ever again."

"So did you try to get her back after it happened?"

Greg nodded. "I begged her. I told her it had been a one-night deal, and a stupid mistake, and that it would never happen again."

"Maxine didn't believe you."

"I slept with her sister, Mel. How could she believe in me ever again? She has zero tolerance for cheating, but for me to have cheated with her sister? The apple of the family's eye?"

Greg shook his head. "Maxine told me she hated my guts and that she'd never forgive me. I wanted her back more than anything. She asked me how many other women I'd screwed and made me do every test in the book: STDs, HIV, you name it. She told me she'd kill me if I'd given her sister anything. The results came back clean, but she still wouldn't touch me. Said she'd never touch me again. She shut me out of her life. She threw everything I owned on the front lawn and changed the locks. I'm sure you heard about the night I beat on the front door, begging her to forgive me. To give me a chance."

Melanie bit her lip and nodded. "I'm sorry."

Greg exhaled harshly. "As if I didn't feel guilty enough, Erika went crazy when I told her I didn't plan to leave Maxine for her. You know about that, right? Everyone in town knows."

"They say Erika had a nervous breakdown because of you, but..." Melanie shook her head.

"You don't believe them?"

Melanie's blue gaze bored into his. "No, I don't. Erika ran off to Miami afterward, but I refuse to believe it had anything to do with you. I think she used what happened with you as an excuse to leave Wyndham Shores. She hated it here. She'd always been spoiled rotten, and she'd been wild and restless and desperate for attention. She loved playing the victim."

"Mel—"

"It's true. You weren't the first guy she'd hooked up with."

Greg lowered his head. "Everyone in town thinks I drove her to that nervous breakdown she had when I dropped her."

"And you feel guilty about that."

"Of course. It kills me to think about how much I hurt Erika, too."

Melanie drew in a slow breath. "If it makes you feel better, last I heard she's doing fine. Working in some club and partying harder than ever. I even heard she's engaged to some rich guy. Trust me, she's okay."

Greg slowly nodded. It didn't ease the guilt much. "Erika's parents were devastated when she left town. I know the family hasn't been the same. Now, with both of their daughters gone—"

"Erika didn't plan to live in Wyndham Shores forever, anyway."

Greg drew in a breath. He still felt responsible for devastating both sisters and ripping the family apart.

"I know you cared about Maxine," Melanie said. "You were honest with her and you asked for her forgiveness afterward."

"But I did the one thing she could never forgive. We'd always promised to work things out, but even after all we'd been through, and all the trouble we went through to get together in the first place, she wouldn't forgive me. And I didn't blame her."

"Greg—"

"I ran into Maxine in the grocery store last time I was here. She had a cart full of groceries that day. She always loved to cook. She had all this fresh stuff, and I had these stupid…Hungry Man frozen dinners. Kind of summed up our different lives at that point. I was so stupid that night. I wanted to fix my mistakes and make her forgive me. I reminded her about how happy we were and how I gave her everything and still wanted to, but it was too late. She told me she was marrying Allen and that she'd never go back to me. She said the sight of me made her sick."

"I'm sorry," Melanie whispered.

"It's tough having someone you love say that."

She bit her lip, concern filling her eyes.

"I tried to eat the microwave dinner that night but couldn't. I don't think I ate for a week after that. No appetite. I kept thinking about how I'd destroyed our life together."

"That was the lowest point, right? That day at the store?"

He nodded. "After that, I picked myself up and went to work. Threw myself into it."

"And then you got hurt."

"Yeah. The Navy shipped me out soon after that. Some guys took hostages on a fishing boat in the Indian Ocean. I ended up taking a shell."

Melanie nodded. "I'm so sorry. I heard that you got injured, but I wasn't sure how. I didn't know you'd saved lives."

He grimaced. "I'm no hero, believe me. It was just part of the job."

"What you did was very brave."

"I'm not so brave, Mel."

"You're hurting. I can tell."

"It feels okay most of the time. It aches a little on days like today when it's humid."

"How long ago did you get shot?"

"Eight months ago."

Melanie nodded. "I wish it hadn't happened."

"I'd do it again if I had to."

Melanie nodded again.

It felt good to talk about what happened. He'd never discussed it with anyone, but somehow he felt comfortable telling Mel. For the first time in a long time, he felt like someone was listening instead of judging. And for a minute, he allowed himself to enjoy her company.

***

"Nice night," Melanie said while they came outside the diner.

She reached for Greg's hand. He looked at her like that surprised him, but he squeezed her hand in his. She wished she could protect him from the unkind words of everyone in town. She knew he didn't need her protection, but she still wanted to show him he at least had one friend around here.

"It'll be dark in a few minutes," Greg said. "Where's your car? I'll walk you to it."

"Oh. I've been walking everywhere. My car's in the shop. Major repairs I can't afford."

He smiled. "You still driving that old beaten-up red Pontiac?"

She nodded. "I'm saving up for something else, but it takes a while."

"Yeah, I know how that is." He nodded toward the harbor. "Come on, I'll give you a ride home."

"I can walk—"

"No way, Mel. I'll drive you. If anything happened to you—"

She cocked her head and grinned. "In Wyndham Shores? I don't think so."

"Still—"

"Okay, fine. A ride would be great."

They walked to the parking lot and Greg came around and held the passenger door of his truck open for her.

"Thanks." She climbed in.

He shut the door and then came around to the driver's side, then hopped into the cab. "This thing needs repairs, but it's hardly worth the money to fix it."

"You still have your house, right?"

He nodded and started the engine. "I keep the truck parked around the side under a tarp when I'm not here. It keeps the weather off it."

"You're lucky you still have your house."

"Yeah." He steered out of the lot. "Somewhere to call home. It's hot out tonight. Want me to turn the air on?"

She shook her head. "It's fine. I like the night air coming in through the windows."

"Me, too. Where do you live?"

"The apartments on Cherrybrook Lane. You know where they are?"

"Sure."

Melanie stared out the window while they drove. "This town is so strange."

"Yeah. I know."

Yet she'd stayed. Month and month and year after year. She'd often thought about going somewhere else and doing something different with her life, but she'd never had the confidence to take the plunge and leave.

"Does it feel different to you, after being gone for a while?" she asked.

"No. Nothing changes around here. It's like someone pressed the freeze button twenty years ago."

She nodded. "I know what you mean. Sometimes I feel like someone pressed the freeze button on my life. Like I haven't accomplished much."

"I know that's not true," he said. "Besides, if you'd already accomplished everything you wanted to, there'd be no reason to rush out of bed in the morning ready to face the day, right?"

"True."

When they reached her garden-style apartment complex, on a grassy hill covered with trees, Greg pulled into a parking spot. He got out and ran around to open the passenger side door for her.

Greg looked up at her building. "So this is it."

She nodded. She knew it wasn't exactly the height of luxury. A few siding panels hung loose on the outside of the building, and shingles on the roof needed replacing. The wooden decks on each apartment needed a good cleaning and the railings had begun to rust. The place had worn down over the years but management never expressed any interest in fixing it up.

"It's nice," Greg said.

She laughed. "It's not nice. It's…affordable."

"I'll see you to the door."

"Okay."

The thought of Greg being in her apartment felt strange. She hadn't expected him or any other company tonight. She'd often dreamed about being alone with him in her apartment, but she'd never thought it would ever become reality. What would he think of her hand-me-down furniture and cheap knick-knacks covering the shelves?

She scooped up a pile of magazines and newspapers from the worn plaid couch and set them on the side table. "Sorry it's so messy in here."

"It's fine."

She'd decorated the living room in pinks and reds. It was girly, but she'd relished the opportunity to decorate however she wanted, and this was her style. The couch and two armchairs faced the small flat screen TV. The TV set on a storage chest and she wasn't sure when she'd have the money for an actual stand.

"Have a seat," she said. "Make yourself at home."

Greg sat.

"We didn't have dessert," she said. "Would you like something? I've got part of a pie from Lonnie's Bakery. The best apple pie in town."

Greg rubbed his palms on his jeans. "Sure. Pie sounds good."

Melanie went into the kitchen, grabbed the pie from the fridge and cut two slices. She brought the two plates over.

"Thanks," he said.

She sat next to him on the couch, and she could feel the loneliness coming off of him. It was almost as intense as hers. No one had treated him fairly, and he'd deserved better.

She watched him take a few bites of the pie.

Unlike most guys, he hadn't hit on her just because he had the opportunity. Even now he made no moves on her, and it drove her crazy. Did he find her attractive at all?

"Let me see your side," she said.

"It's fine."

"I saw you touching it this afternoon. You're in pain, right?"

"It's not that bad."

She set her plate on the side table. "I could take a look. Make sure it's not still infected."

He set the pie aside and lifted his shirt. She saw where the bullet had gone in and pressed her fingers against it.

"Does it hurt?" she asked.

"Off and on."

"There's no heat. That's good. No infection."

"Didn't think so. The Navy gave me a complete bill of health. A complete physical. According to them, I can't get any healthier. And this thing's healed all the way."

"That's good. But it still hurts, right?"

"Sometimes." He drew in a labored breath. "I guess the pain will go away eventually."

"Does Maxine know you got shot?" She wondered if his ex even cared.

"She might have heard the rumors."

"But she never said anything to you about it. She never expressed any concern."

"No. I didn't expect her to."

Melanie drew in a breath. "From what I saw, she didn't treat you right."

"She was angry."

"I mean before that."

"Maybe not. But at this point, it doesn't matter. She has no intention of communicating with me. Ever. She thinks I'm scum."

Melanie's eyes met his. "I don't."

Greg looked at her like he didn't know quite how to process that.

"Do you still love her?"

"I think about her, but it's more because of…what I did wrong. I know she doesn't love me, and I can't keep loving her when I know that."

"Have you dated anyone since your divorce?" Melanie asked.

He shook his head.

She shot him a mischievous smile. "Kissed anyone?"

He laughed and shook his head again. "Actually, I, uh…haven't. Guess I've had other things on my mind."

"Sounds a little lonely. Did you miss it?"

"Kissing?"

She nodded.

He laughed softly. "Who wouldn't?"

Melanie leaned toward him. Greg moved closer but hesitated, as if unsure whether he should bring his mouth to hers. She pressed her lips to his, testing him out, seeing if he'd respond. He did. They kissed, their mouths melding into one another. She parted her lips and felt his mouth open against hers in response. Then he sank his tongue into her mouth and shifted closer to her.

He deepened the kiss further. She felt a twinge between her thighs and moaned softly in her throat when his tongue rubbed against hers. Then he pulled away.

"Mel, what's going on here?" he asked.

"Kissing. Do you like it?"

He looked at her. "Yeah. I like it a lot."

"Me, too. No one would guess you're out of practice."

He laughed quietly.

She grew serious, her smile fading. "I've always wondered what it would be like to kiss you."

"And now—"

"You've exceeded my expectations."

He smiled. "Is that right?"

She nodded. Melanie leaned in and kissed him some more, and Greg placed one hand on her hip and explored the curve of her. His other hand went to her breast, touching her lightly through her T-shirt.

She slid her lips over his throat, exploring the rough texture where the stubble was beginning to come in. Even after their long day he smelled like aftershave. It mixed with his unique masculine scent and she couldn't get enough. She licked the five-o'clock shadow on his neck and explored the texture of the softer skin below. She ran her hand down his chest, feeling the hard muscles draw in beneath her hands.

Then she placed her hand over the bulge in his crotch, rubbing lightly while they kissed. She felt him harden through his jeans.

Greg touched her hand. "What's happening here, Mel?"

She licked her lips, her breath coming fast, her heart pounding. "I want you. But you're not feeling it."

"I'm feeling it, but I haven't even taken you out on a real date."

"I'd like you to take me out," she said.

"Tomorrow night. Eight o'clock."

"Yes."

"Mel, whether we go out or not, I can't give you what you need," Greg said. "A meaningful relationship is the last thing I'm after right now."

"Who said anything about a meaningful relationship?"

"What are you saying?" Greg asked.

"I'm saying we could have this for now. If you'll let me."

"I've got nothing to give you."

"I have nothing to give you, either." She kissed him again. "Take off your shirt," she murmured in his ear.

He did. She slowly kissed her way down his bare chest, then his stomach, as she went. Then she slid to her knees on the carpet and reached for the zipper of his jeans.

"Mel."

Her gaze met his. "I know no one's done this for you in a while. You haven't let them. Have you?"

"No." It came out a harsh groan.

"I get the feeling that because of what happened with Maxine, you think you don't deserve any love or pleasure ever again. Is that right?"

"Yeah. Maybe."

"I don't believe it's true. I think you deserve both."

"Everyone wants to punish me—"

"I don't."

He touched her cheek, his gaze meeting hers. "I think you're alone."

"I don't care. Everyone else is wrong," she said quietly. "Look, I didn't plan this and this isn't how I pictured my day ending when I woke up this morning. But sometimes the unexpected happens, and it turns out to be something good."

"Guess I never thought about that."

"I want to do this for you. You said you've got a clean bill of health, right?"

He nodded. "Squeaky clean."

"So we can…take it all the way…and there's no danger of…anything."

"That's right."

"So we've got nothing to worry about, then, do we?"

He shook his head. "I'm clean. But Mel—"

Her eyes locked with his as she slid the zipper down.

***

Blood surged through Greg's veins and his heart pumped wildly in his chest. He couldn't let her do this.

Greg pulled her up his body and bought his mouth to hers. He kissed her, trying to distract her for a while. He wanted to make her forget about blowing him when they'd barely gone out on a real date. Going to the diner tonight didn't count as a date.

She couldn't know what she was doing. Her mouth felt hot and sweet and giving and he slid his tongue against hers. Bad move. It excited him more.

She slipped her hand into his boxer briefs while they kissed. He had to stop her.

"Mel…"

Her hazy eyes met his gaze. "I want you in my mouth," she whispered.

He almost came at just the thought of being in her mouth, but knew this was all wrong. But before he could protest, she knelt before him and shifted her weight, getting comfortable.

"Mel, wait."

"Okay. I don't want you to do something you don't want."

"Yeah." He swallowed, his heart pounding in his chest. "We should wait."

She pulled away and sat back on her heels, looking hurt and rejected. "I understand."

"Mel…"

"I'm sorry, Greg. This is too fast, right? Maybe another time. Maybe after you take me on that date."

"Yeah. Okay."

Greg tried to get air in his lungs and clear his foggy brain. Shit. He couldn't think straight anymore.

He'd be crazy to turn this down. Mel wanted to do this, didn't she? Maybe she was right. Sometimes the unexpected happened and it turns out to be a good thing. He hadn't had many good things happen lately. He tried to relax.

"Okay." His heart pounded. "Let's go for it. If you're sure you want to do this."

Her eyes shimmered as her gaze met his. "I'm sure."

His breath came fast and furious. He didn't know if this was the right thing or not, or if he was making a big mistake, but leaned back, giving her room. His legs quaked and he stifled a groan when she pulled out his hard cock out of his boxer briefs. Just the feel of her fingers on him had him crazy, and every muscle in his body shook with anticipation. Would he survive her mouth on him?

She leaned forward and touched her parted lips against the bottom of his shaft. He groaned as she slid upward, licking him the whole way. Then she slowly ran her tongue around the crown.

"You're big," she murmured.

"I know. Too big." He tried to hold onto what little control her had left while she licked the sweet spot under the head. "That feels great," he groaned. "But you don't have to—"

She licked off the bead of moisture that had formed at the tip and then slipped the head into her mouth. She sank all the way down his shaft, opening wide, working hard to take him all in. He felt like an ass that it excited him, but after the pain of the past eighteen months, mental and physical, finally experiencing pleasuring again drove him out of his mind.

She closed her eyes and slowly sucked him in and out, settling into a rhythm while he shuddered with pleasure beneath her. Each thrust of her mouth, each swirl of her tongue around him drove him closer to madness.

"Melanie."

The last of the air in his lungs rushed out. He wanted to keep watching the beautiful sight of her. Of him disappearing into her mouth over and over again. Pure heaven. But he was too far gone and he leaned his head back against the back of the couch, squeezing his eyes shut.

He needed her to move faster, but let her set the pace. Almost delirious, his hips moved involuntarily beneath him but he forced himself to keep his thrusts shallow.

"Mel, I'm about to—" He blew out a short, rough breath, slowly losing control. The air felt hot in his lungs and he was so close. "You'd better stop."

She ignored him, then wrapped her hand around the bottom of his shaft, stroking in a tight rhythm while she pleasured the head with her mouth. He lost himself in ecstasy.

He leaned up. "Mel—"

She moaned and increased her pace. His hands threaded in her hair. He tried to be gentle, but he needed it fast and hard. He couldn't think. Couldn't move. His mind went blank and all he could do was lie there and let her take him over the edge. He stiffened beneath her, about to come in her mouth—

He jerked and groaned with his climax. Lightning bolts of pleasure blinded him as he released his seed in burst after hot burst. Their gazes locked as she swallowed, and the fact that she'd do that for him sent another shock of pleasure through him, then another. She eagerly took every drop of his desire, and then finished him off with a few last soft slow strokes of her tongue.

He gasped for air. He couldn't move. His body lay limp, paralyzed while he drew in heavy gulps of air.

She slowly kissed her way back up his chest, each touch of her soft, sweet mouth turning him on again. Just the thought of what she'd done to him blew his mind, and he struggled to come back to earth.

Her eyes were hazy and her chest rose and fell with heavy breaths. She was shaking by the time her body covered his. He kissed her and felt her breathing hard.

"You okay?" He drew her into his lap.

She nodded, her hand softly stroking over his chest. "I've wanted to do that for you for so long."

He massaged her back with one hand. So this is what people meant by the term guilty pleasure. A lot of pleasure followed by a lot of guilt. He drew in a heavy breath. "I shouldn't have let you do that."

"You didn't like it?"

"Like it? It was incredible."

But sex always had a price. A price he couldn't pay right now.

"Good. I hoped you'd like it."

"We shouldn't have—"

"I know it was too fast. But I couldn't help it. While you were with Maxine, I never would have made a move on you. And I might not ever get you single again."

"I'm not planning on hooking up with anyone."

"But after you leave I might not ever see you again."

"That would be okay, wouldn't it? You deserve more than me."

She drew in a gulp of air, as if considering that.

"Sure you're all right?" he asked.

"Fine, I'm just…turned on," she said.

He breathed hard. He'd do something about that as soon as he could move. They lay there for a long time until their breathing settled into a rhythm together.

"Take off your bra," he said finally, resting his chin against the top of her head. "I want to see your breasts."

She took her bra off and straddled him on the couch. Beautiful. Her nipples were small and perfect. He stared at her breasts before taking both in his hands. She gasped while he stroked his thumbs over her nipples.

Face to face now, he leaned in and kissed her, tasting the sweetness of her lips, his tongue sinking into the depths of her mouth. Then he kissed his way down to her breasts, needing them in his mouth. He opened his mouth over her, teasing and licking the hard point of one nipple and then the other, using his tongue to excite her before drawing her as deeply into her mouth as he could. He suckled her.

She whimpered. "Greg."

His mouth found her other breast while his hand slid down into her shorts and inside her panties. She gasped as he traced her folds with the tip of his finger. She was so wet, and just the thought of her being so turned on from sucking him made him half-hard again.

He teased her inner lips with his fingers, using the lightest touch he could before sinking two fingers inside her. He stroked her channel, her muscles contracting around him before he sank his fingers in deeper, eager to bring her to release. His thumb found her clit, and he lightly stroked until she moved wildly against him. Before long her felt her tremors, her tightening around his fingers. He kissed her mouth, his tongue moving against hers in time with his fingers, swallowing her cries of pleasure.

She thrust her hips and he tried to keep contact with her clit. Gradually she stopped moving and fell limply against him, her head resting on his shoulder.

He held her while her breathing slowly came back to normal.

"I needed that," she said softly.

He buried his face in the crook of her neck. The skin was so soft there. "I barely did anything for you—"

"Next time," she said.

"Definitely next time."

She looked up at him and grinned. "I like the sound of there being a next time. How about some no strings attached sexual healing? For both of us, while you're here in town."

"No strings, huh?"

"No strings. We could be together until you leave," Melanie said. "I think we both need this."

Greg shifted uncomfortably beneath her. "I'm not into using someone and leaving."

"You wouldn't be using me. I need you, too."

She looked at him with a pleading look in her eyes. She looked so sweet. He knew he should resist her but had no idea how he'd manage it.

"Okay." He swallowed hard. "We can do that."

She nodded.

For a second he panicked. What had he just agreed to? Sexual healing with Mel? He needed something, but it was unfair to her to agree to this when he knew it could never be just sexual healing. Sex always complicated things. And why would she want to be with a guy like him, anyway?

He needed to get out of here, and fast. "I should get going, Mel."

She nodded. "I guess we both have to be at work early in the morning."

"Yeah."

She climbed off of him and they got to their feet.

They both put their clothes back on, and she took the pie plates into the kitchen. He watched her go. She was beautiful. Beyond beautiful. He watched the sweep of her neck, her legs.

He stood there like a moron, not knowing whether to stay or go. She came back out into the living room and he gave her one last kiss on the mouth.

"Thanks for…everything," he said.

She nodded, looking shy. "See you tomorrow."

Greg slowly walked out the door. Guilt filled him. He couldn't help thinking he'd stolen pleasure and it made him beyond an ass. So much for staying out of trouble. It hadn't taken him long to ruin that plan.

He didn't dare think he could actually start anything with Melanie. This had been a huge mistake.

He went out to the car, feeling more lost and confused than ever.

***

The next morning, Melanie dreaded going to work. How would she face Greg again? She dreaded it even more when she came down the dock and saw Greg already hard at work on Lady Luck. Her mouth went dry and she wondered what he'd think of her. What did she expect him to think? She'd given him a blowjob after they'd barely gotten reacquainted and then offered him sexual healing when they'd barely gone out on date.

Chalk it up to being overcome with lust and totally out of control. The crazy part was she'd liked giving him a blowjob. It had turned her on like nothing ever had, and the thought of doing it again for him made her wet. But something told her it had been a one-time deal, despite the offer for sexual healing they'd discussed last night.

After what she'd done, he probably thought of her as trash, just like everyone else in town, and he wouldn't want anything more to do with her. If they'd had a chance for some kind of relationship, or for them to develop into something, she'd ruined it last night.

"Hi," Greg said.

"Hi."

His gaze met hers for a second while she walked past him. He looked at her with more than just casual interest, like he at least acknowledged something had happened between them last night, but she turned away.

Melanie worked in silence all morning, and sighed at her own stupidity. She'd moved way too fast. She always moved too fast, and then wondered why she scared guys off. Wondered why they didn't call the next day. It had been a stupid move, and she couldn't expect anything from him. She wouldn't.

***

Things were going to be awkward between them, all because of her.

At lunchtime she brought back a bag of takeout from the diner for Greg and Emmett.

"Mel—" Greg said.

She handed him the bag, barely able to look at him. "I should…I should get back to work." She brushed past him.

Emmett came up to her later. "Mel. Something going on?"

"Sorry?"

"With you and fly boy."

Melanie shook her head.

"Good. Because you're looking at him funny this afternoon, and I thought maybe something was going on."

"No."

"Keep it that way. Don't hang out with that guy," Emmett said. "He's trouble."

"It's all right, Emmett."

She appreciated Emmett's concern and the way he protected her. She didn't have a lot of people in her life willing to protect her. But she didn't want his protection. She didn't want anyone telling her who she could spend time with.

***

Greg watched Melanie work. She'd avoided him all day.

He scratched his cheek. Last night baffled him. He didn't know what to make of what happened. He didn't know what hit him or what had come over her.

He stared at the sweet, graceful line of her neck.

The softness of her mouth. The pleasure she'd given him with that mouth had been insane, and he wanted to do the same for her.

The sadness in her eyes…he'd like to see her happy and flushed with pleasure. He'd barely noticed her pleasure last night because he'd been so wrapped up in his own. She'd come with his fingers in her, but he'd like to feel her spasm around his hard cock next time, while he thrust in and out of her. He went hard at the thought and had to think about counting pushups before someone noticed the bulge in his pants.

Melanie. She'd made him laugh yesterday, and no one had made him laugh in a while. She intrigued him, not just sexually, and he wanted to find out more about her.

Maybe the sexual healing she'd suggested hadn't been such a bad idea. Maybe it could be mutually beneficial.

He finally caught up with her at the end of the day.

"Hey, Mel. Everything okay?"

"Fine."

"You've been ignoring me."

She lowered her head. "What happened last night…I keep thinking about it."

He smiled. "Me, too."

"I'm sorry."

"I'm not."

"I got carried away."

"I did, too."

Her gaze met his. "We said some things in the heat of the moment, but you don't owe me sexual healing."

"You don't owe me, either, Mel. But were you planning on talking to me ever again?"

"Maybe we should just work together. Forget the rest."

"Is that what you want to do?" he asked.

She shook her head. "I don't know."

He didn't. Maybe he should forget about it and chalk it up to a crazy mistake, but he didn't want to. "I'd like to take you out tonight."

She glanced up at him, her eyes brightening. "You would?"

"I promised you a date," he said. "I want to take you somewhere nice."

The light in her eyes dimmed. "You don't have to take me out just because we talked about it yesterday."

"That's not why—"

"You're under no obligation."

"This isn't about obligation. I want to spend some time with you. How's seven o'clock? I'll pick you up at your place."

She bit her lip and drew in a little breath, thinking

it over. "You sure you still want to do this?

"Positive."

He finally got a smile out of her.

"Okay," she said. "Seven o'clock."

He smiled. "Great. See you then."

Melanie headed out for the day, and he stayed behind to finish cleaning up for the night. Who knew where this was headed or where tonight would end up. He was getting himself into trouble all over again, but couldn't stop himself.

***

Melanie rushed home to her apartment and showered, eager to clean herself up for their date. She'd felt sloppy last night in shorts and a T-shirt, and she reveled in the chance to dress up and feel pretty tonight.

She chose a short little maroon dress that showed off a little cleavage, and slipped into a pair of black pumps. With her skin clean and her hair smelling of shampoo instead of sea air and dirt, she felt wonderful.

She blow-dried her hair and left it flowing in waves over her shoulders, and then put on her favorite shade of lipstick and a little eye shadow. Then she slipped in a pair of silver hoop earrings and put on the matching bracelet. She dabbed a tiny bit of perfume on her wrists, and examined herself in the mirror. She smoothed her hands down the front of her dress and smiled. Not bad.

Who knew what the night held? Deep down she knew Greg might be going out with her only to fulfill his supposed obligation, and it dampened her spirits. She couldn't think too much of this, or hope he'd invited her out because he actually enjoyed spending time with her.

She took one last look in the mirror as the doorbell rang.

Greg smiled when she opened the door, looking dapper in a pair of black dress pants and blue dress shirt. "Ready?"

She nodded. She could hardly believe she was going out with him, and he'd dressed up, like this was special to him. She smelled the faint trace of aftershave, something rich and masculine, and she wanted to bury her face in his neck and lose herself in him.

Greg pulled into the parking lot of Murray's, the nicest restaurant in town. It seated only about twenty people at small wooden tables overlooking the water. Tourists fought for reservations for months.

"We can't eat here," she said.

"You don't like seafood?"

"We need a reservation months in advance."

He pulled the key out and came around to the passenger side door. "Don't worry about a thing."

He helped her out of the truck, and she couldn't help but be pleased as his gaze roamed over her cleavage, checking her out as she stepped out of the cab. His gaze dropped down her body to her legs, then back up to the swell of her breasts. She hoped he liked what he saw.

She put her arm in his as they walked into the restaurant, and shot him an incredulous look when they went inside and the maître-d seated them right away at a table for two overlooking the water.

"How did you—?"

He grinned. "I called early this morning. They had a cancellation. We got lucky."

"I'll say." And she hoped they'd both get lucky in more ways than one tonight.

As they sat, Melanie looked around at tea lights casting a romantic glow at each table. She couldn't remember the last time she'd eaten at a place with white linen tablecloths, a gleaming hardwood floor and fine custom made furniture. She unfolded her crisp white napkin, set it in her lap, and tried to relax.

"I can't believe this place. It's so beautiful," she said.

Greg set his napkin in his lap. "Glad you like it."

"I've never eaten here."

"I find it hard to believe no one's ever taken you here."

"Well, believe it."

"The food's supposed to be incredible."

"So I've heard," Melanie said.

A date with Greg. Who would have thought?
When she'd been back in high school she would have
died to have a night like this. She'd longed for a little
romance back then, and over the years she'd quit expecting it. She decided to savor every second tonight.

They ate a delicious meal of lobster, crab cakes
and salad. When the bill arrived she offered to go Dutch,
but Greg adamantly refused. She felt bad. She knew he
wasn't making bank from either the Navy or Emmett, but
he insisted it was his treat.

After dinner they walked along the water, the salty
smell of the ocean surrounding them.

Greg touched the small of her back, making her
shiver. "The temperature dropped. You cold?"

She shook her head. "It's a beautiful night."

She looked up at the stars filling the night sky.

He stuffed his hands in his pockets while they
walked. "Mel, how come you're nice to me when everyone else in this town practically wants me dead?"

"I've always liked you."

"Even after you heard what I did to Maxine?"

She nodded. "I knew there was more to the story
than just you cheating because you were a jerk. I know
there's a story behind what happened. You're not a
cheating jerk."

"Don't think too highly of me, Mel."

"Do you remember this night, about a year and a

half ago right before you left the last time? You'd gone to Luddy's Tavern."

"What night was that?"

"Maxine's brother Shawn had been heckling you at the bar, calling you all kinds of names, and when you tried to leave, he came after you."

He groaned at the memory. "Ah. That night."

She touched his cheek in the moonlight. She could see a faint trace of the tiny scar where his teeth had gone through his cheek when Shawn had socked him. Greg had bled all over the place. She'd never forget that night.

"I saw what Shawn did. I saw him punch you so hard in the jaw…" She shook her head. "And then he kicked you—"

Greg gave a humorless laugh. "In the balls."

"He knocked the wind out of you and you could hardly breathe. I thought he'd killed you. I wanted you to fight back. I wanted to see you punch his lights out, but you didn't. Why not?"

"I didn't want to fight him."

"You would have been defending yourself. You could have punched him right back."

He shrugged. "Maybe I thought I deserved what he did."

Her jaw dropped. "How can you think that, Greg? Of course you didn't deserve it."

"I hurt both of his sisters. He told me I'd ripped their family apart. He was paying me back."

She shook her head. "What he did wasn't right."

"No. But he thought I deserved it. I took it and paid the price for what I did. I figured if it made him feel better to do that—"

Tears formed in Melanie's eyes. "You didn't deserve to be treated that way."

"Maybe I did."

"You could have hurt him," Melanie said. "Shawn talks big but underneath all the talk, he's a wimp. You could have taken that man down with no problem, but you chose not to."

"That's right. I wasn't going to take him out. It wouldn't have been right."

"Always the peacekeeper, aren't you?"

"I guess so."

She'd wept for Greg that night and wanted to weep for him now.

"I'd hurt that family enough," Greg said softly. "Why add to the hurt?"

Melanie drew in a breath. "I wish you would realize how wrong Shawn was. How wrong Maxine was to throw you away. If you were mine—"

She drew in a gasp and lowered her head, wishing she could take back the words. She hadn't meant for that part to come out. But he didn't press her to explain what she'd meant.

"Thanks, Mel. Thanks for caring."

She nodded, and then slowly moved in and kissed his cheek. She pressed her mouth against the tiny scar she wished would disappear. But it would be there for life.

"Did last night surprise you?" She watched his face, trying to catch his expression.

"Yeah. It did. Took me by surprise."

"Me, too. But I don't regret it."

His gaze locked with hers and his mouth became a firm line. "I don't, either."

She wanted to kiss those delicious looking lips of his, but she would wait until they got somewhere alone.

***

Greg drove Melanie back to her apartment, and he wondered if she wanted him to come in. Did she want to sleep with him? He definitely wanted to sleep with her tonight, and that was another surprise. His need for her had simmered all night but now it had gone up to a boil. Who would have thought?

After last night, he figured she'd be up for a slow, seductive session in her bedroom. If she wanted him at all, she would probably want him to make love to her nice and easy and tender. But as soon as they got in her bedroom Melanie stripped off his shirt and pants, then licked and kissed her way down his naked chest. He was rock hard by the time she knelt in front of him.

"Mel, wait—"

She ran her hands over his thighs and his stomach, exciting him more than he thought possible. Then she cupped his balls in her hand and traced her tongue lightly over them. By the time she wrapped her lips over the head, he was so far gone he thought he'd explode any second. She sucked him hard, then slow, then hard again, and he pumped into her mouth. So much for slow and easy.

Blood surged through his veins while he watched the erotic sight of her pleasuring him. But he couldn't come yet. He wanted more for her.

"Mel, wait." He drew her to her feet.

"I want you to come in my mouth."

"Next time."

"I liked it when you did that—"

"Me, too. We'll do that again later. Right now I have to be inside you," he said. "I need you on the bed."

Mel nodded. Her cheeks flushed and from the passionate look on her face, she wanted that as much as he did.

He'd brought condoms with him tonight, just in case. He grabbed one and sheathed himself while she slid her panties down her legs and stepped out of them. Then she climbed onto the bed and slipped the skirt of her dress over her hips. She urged him to join her on the bed, then lay back and opened her thighs. He moved between them and she guided him inside her.

"Mel, you sure you're ready?"

She nodded. "I've wanted you inside me for years." She panted. "I never thought it would happen."

"It's happening."

He slid into the soft, wet heat of her inch by inch slowly, giving her time to adjust to his girth. The feel of being inside her was like nothing he'd ever known. He squeezed his eyes shut and wondered if this was only a dream.

"You're so tight, Mel," he said.

"Do you like that I'm tight?"

"Yes." He thrust halfway in. "I know I'm big—"

"You are. Give me a minute to relax, and you can go in further. I want to take all of you."

He groaned at the thought. Then he surprised both of them by pulling out of her. She whimpered.

"Lose the dress," he said. "I want you naked. I want to see your breasts. *All of you.* I want to see myself going inside you without the dress in the way."

"Yes," she gasped.

She took a moment to strip off the dress and bra, and his hard cock pulsed at the sight of her naked body. Of her spreading her legs for him again. He kissed her belly and then ran his fingers over her labia, soft folds that welcomed him, beckoning him. He got between her thighs again, unable to wait another second. He looked down and watched himself disappear into her heat.

The hot, wet of her inner muscles gripped him as he slipped in further, and it was more pleasure than he could stand. He wanted to slip further into her, but didn't know if he'd hurt her. She breathed hard.

"You feel so good," she whispered.

He gruffly muttered something back against her earlobe. Wasn't sure what it was.

He pulled out a little, giving her time to adjust and get ready for all of his length. She pressed her mouth against his ear.

"Go in all the way," she whispered, the words like a soft caress on his neck.

Already on the brink of orgasm, he shuddered as he sank in further. But he breathed in a slow breath and forced himself back from the edge of ecstasy. Melanie wanting to take all of him was more than he could stand.

Her mouth opened, wet against his shoulder, and she licked him, her tongue swirling over his skin.

"You're killing me, Mel."

"Come on. All the way," she murmured.

That little bit of waiting had given her enough time to adjust, because this time he buried himself to the root. He filled her totally and completely, and they both groaned with the pleasure of him filling her with everything he had.

Balls aching with the need for release, he stayed there for a minute, buried all the way in her, as deep as he could go. He ground his pelvis against hers and thought he'd die with pleasure.

He held still until they were both shaking from head to toe and neither could stand it any longer. He pulled out slowly, knowing if he moved too fast this would all be over, and he wanted to savor every millisecond.

She thrust her hips up to his as he sank back into her. They found a rhythm together, him giving her several shallow thrusts before sinking all the way in, then several shallow thrusts again. She panted with need. Her eyes hazed over with pleasure, so he figured she liked it.

"Almost there," she murmured.

"Come on, Mel. Come with me inside you."

"*Yes*," she said.

Her breathing quickened and he felt her trembling as he moved in and out of her. He thrust deep once more and she tightened around his hard length, gasping as her tremors began. She squeezed all around him and he couldn't hold back much longer.

He savored that brief second as his own climax approached, and groaned with ecstasy as he came in a series of hard, hot bursts inside her.

Afterward, Melanie settled up against him. "That

was a great end to the date."

He stroked her hair. "I'll say."

"You can stay here tonight," she said.

He almost panicked. Everything in him told him to get up and run out of here as fast as he could. They'd gotten too close, and he couldn't handle this. But how much of an ass would he be if he did that?

Greg drew her closer into his arms. He should stay. And he had to admit he'd missed this. He'd missed making love and enjoying the pleasures of being with a woman. Someone who might feel something for him other than hatred.

For the first time in a long time, he felt like someone new. His heart had lifted. Was it possible he could have a fresh start? Start over? Would he ever have a relationship with anyone again, or even be close to someone?

Maybe he didn't deserve a second chance, and he'd never get that second chance. But for the first time in a long time, he wondered if he might be able to have one.

Chapter Three

Melanie met Amelia for coffee on Saturday morning in her tiny coffee shop near the docks. The place served mostly locals and had only four tables, so most people grabbed a cup and went on to work afterward.

Amelia was cute and petite, with gobs of curly blond ringlets and eyelashes for days. She'd once been full of dreams of moving to New York City to become a dancer, but instead, she'd run herself ragged running the shop after her mom died three years ago. Melanie stopped in a few times a week to catch up, and she'd done her best to try and convince her friend to slow down. Amelia had finally hired some help a few months ago, but she still ran herself ragged. Melanie wondered if it was to avoid having to deal with other parts of her life.

Amelia scrubbed down the counter and started two fresh pots of coffee.

"You sure you have time to talk this morning?" Melanie asked.

"Of course. Let's sit." Amelia called into the back room. "Carolina, can you cover for me for a few minutes?"

The redheaded teenager came out from the back room, tying an apron around her waist. "Sure."

"We'll just be a few minutes," Amelia said.

Carolina nodded, and Melanie and Amelia found a table in the empty shop. But it wasn't empty for long.

As soon as they sat down, Greg and one of his Navy buddies, Craig, walked through the door. Greg had mentioned that Craig had volunteered to help Emmett out for a day laying in some new hardwood on Lady Luck.

The two guys chatted with Carolina as she served them coffee. Craig laughed and flirted with her, but Greg looked serious. Melanie had to admit that pleased her. She had no hold on him, but she still would have been incredibly jealous if he'd flirted.

Greg turned and gave a quick look back at Melanie while they waited. Then he nodded to her, coffee cup in hand, and gave her a knowing wink before he and Craig headed out the door.

Melanie's face flushed with pleasure. The look in his eyes acknowledged what they'd shared, and confirmed that she wasn't just some woman off the street. It hadn't gone unnoticed by Amelia.

"What was that about?" Amelia asked.

Melanie shook her head. "Nothing."

"Huh." Amelia looked at Melanie over the rim of her coffee cup and took a sip. "You and Greg. Who would have thought?"

Melanie gave her a furtive smile.

"Something's going on. That was no ordinary look he gave you."

"We're, uh…friends."

Amelia nodded like she didn't believe that for a second. "Friends. You liked him in high school, didn't you?"

"Who didn't?"

Melanie quit fighting her body's reaction. Her face flushed and she knew she'd gone bright red. All she could think about was what they'd done the night before, and pleasure pulsed in her core at the memory.

She'd been surprised she'd been able to orgasm with Greg inside her. He'd filled her to the hilt, and she'd been surprised there'd been room for her muscles to contract. But they had, gripping him tight. She'd come harder than she ever had in her life, much to her dismay. It had been wild and crazy sex, and Melanie could hardly believe she'd had it with Greg. Maybe she'd made a big mistake, and maybe it had meant nothing to him, but right now happiness flowed through her and she wanted to enjoy it while it lasted.

"Must be going well," Amelia noted.

"I don't know what's happening."

"I'm sure you're giving him more than he deserves." Amelia pursed her lips. "All kinds of sex he doesn't deserve."

"Amelia…"

What did she expect? Amelia had no luck when it came to men, but secretly Melanie suspected it was because she'd grown bitter over the years and pushed away anyone who expressed interest in her.

"Tell me I'm wrong about the sex," Amelia said.

"What does it matter to anyone?"

"He doesn't deserve you." Amelia gave her a disapproving look. "Stay healthy. Use condoms."

"Amelia!"

"You'd better."

"I'm always careful."

"You're a giving woman, and the guys you're with never deserve it. Your stupid ex didn't. I know Greg doesn't, either."

Amelia didn't like it when Melanie slept with someone, so most of the time Melanie kept her mouth shut about it. Amelia always thought Melanie jumped in bed with a guy because she had no respect for herself. Not true. Sure, Melanie had more sexual experience than she would have liked. She'd always wanted to find one man to spend her life with but hadn't known quite how to find him.

Her mother had always been cold, withdrawn, pushing away everyone who dared to try to get close to her. She'd led the life of a nun, and Melanie knew she'd been lonely. Melanie wanted more for herself. She didn't want to live her life fearing men and relationships, so she'd put herself out there. Sex didn't equal love, that was for sure. But she'd figured she'd never find that love unless she put herself out there and made an effort.

"I'll be careful," Melanie said. "You know, it's been a long time since I've had a little romance."

"Romance?" Amelia snorted. "In this town? Mel, don't kid yourself that such a thing exists."

"I'm just saying…it's been a while for me. I haven't met anyone recently that interested me."

"So you're saying I should lay off. Give you a break."

Melanie smiled. "I like him. I like spending time with him."

"He's not back to stay, is he?"

Melanie shook her head. "Shore leave."

"Then where do you think this is headed?" Amelia asked.

"I'm not sure yet."

"It can't go anywhere, Mel. You're going to get hurt."

"I know. That's always the risk."

"You've already been hurt. That jerk you married—"

Melanie stared at her coffee cup. "I know."

"Do yourself a favor and don't fall for Greg," Amelia said. "He won't be sticking around. Don't kid yourself that this is going go somewhere."

Melanie lowered her head. "I won't get my hopes up."

She knew Amelia was right. The words hurt, but maybe she'd needed a dose of reality this morning. No matter what had already happened or would happen, she needed to remember that Greg would be leaving. Did she want to be left with a broken heart?

Still, she couldn't help thinking she wanted to see if they had some sort of chance to see where this might go.

***

Later that day, Emmett showed up at the dock sniffling, his nose red, eyes watery.

"You should take care of that cold. You sound terrible," Greg said.

"I'll be fine."

"Don't let it get worse. Get some rest."

"Can't. I need to take Lady out tomorrow night for a run and make sure she's seaworthy. I've been meaning to do it for weeks."

"Emmett, you're too sick to take her out. Stay home and nurse that cold."

"I need to check—"

"Let me take her out."

Emmett shook his head. "I can't let you do that."

"You know I'll take good care of her," Greg said.

Man, what he wouldn't do to take that boat out by himself without Emmett on his back. It'd be a dream come true. But then again, he wouldn't mind some company.

"How long since you've taken a forty-eight-footer out there all by yourself?"

"I can handle it. Besides, Melanie can come with me and help out."

"No way." Emmett's eyes darkened. "You trying to get her alone so you can make your move on her?" He shook his head. "Not on my watch. I told you to stay away from her. Besides, I need her at the house."

"Yeah, okay," Greg muttered.

But he didn't mean it. He wanted to find a way to take her with him.

"If you take Lady out alone, you know what to check for, right?"

"Of course," Greg assured him. "I'll triple check everything on the list."

"You'd better. If something's wrong I want to know about it and I want it fixed."

"Got it."

Emmett gave in and nodded, and Greg thought the old guy might have even relaxed a little. "I can't believe I'm trusting you with her, fly boy."

Greg gave the old guy's shoulder a squeeze. "You know you can."

Emmett shoved him away. "Get out of here."

But Greg could have sworn he caught a glimmer of amusement in Emmett's eyes while he walked away.

**

Greg finally caught up with Melanie later that day. He hadn't seen her since the coffee shop that morning and Emmett said she'd gone to the wholesale mart for a major shopping run. When he finally saw her walking down the dock, pleasure rushed through him. Yeah, he definitely wanted her to come with him.

"Hey," he said. "Haven't seen you in a while."

She ran a hand through her ponytail. "I had to go shopping for Emmett."

"How'd it go?"

"He let me use his truck. I filled the thing up with supplies. It took me an hour to put everything away at his house."

Greg nodded and scratched his forehead. "Look, I'm sorry I couldn't stop to talk in the coffee shop. I, uh…didn't know how you felt about it. I figured everybody'd be talking if we—"

She nodded. "I know. It's okay."

"Listen, I'm taking Lady Luck out tomorrow on a test run."

Melanie nodded, disappointment on her face. "Emmett told me you'd be taking her out."

"I want you to go with me. I asked Emmett, but he said he needed you."

Melanie nodded. "He's really sick. I'll have to take care of him."

He touched her cheek. "Come with me, Mel."

She gave him a sad smile. "I can't."

He drew in a breath. "Okay. Yeah, I understand."

He wasn't going to make her risk her job because he needed her company. Because he needed sex and kept thinking about all the things they could do on that boat alone.

Surprise registered in her eyes. "You really want me to come with you?"

"Yeah, I would. We'd get some time alone. No one bothering us. No one giving us dirty looks."

Melanie gave him a sad smile. "Sounds wonderful, but…I don't know if it'll work out."

Greg touched her chin. "I promise I'll make it up to when I get back."

A smile brightened her face. "I'd like that."

Greg didn't see her that night, and she didn't call him. He figured they both need the time away from one another. Maybe it was for the best. He couldn't get too attached to her, and he didn't want her getting attached to him, either. They'd part ways and move on with their lives soon enough.

He packed a bag with clothes and toiletries for the next day, ready for an adventure on the boat.

For the past eighteen months all he'd thought about was sailing off alone. No orders to follow. No one on his case, no one in his way, no one looking at him like he was the biggest disappointment of their lives. No one but himself to worry about, alone with his thoughts. It had all sounded perfect. But at the moment none of it sounded that appealing.

For years he'd dreamed about buying a boat of his own and sailing off alone every chance he got. Now he wasn't so sure he even wanted to buy it. Weeks ago he would have treasured the chance to sail off by himself, and thinking about sailing off with Mel was a strange, new experience.

The next morning, Greg arrived at the dock at ten. He got ready to sail, and as he came out from below deck, he saw Melanie running down the dock. His heart flip-flopped in his chest. With that sparkle in her eyes and that smile on her lush lips, she was quite the sight for sore eyes.

He smiled. "Hey."

She smiled right back at him. "Want some company?"

"What happened? I thought Emmett needed you," Greg said.

Her grin widened. "Can you believe it? He gave me the day off. I went to buy him medicine this morning, but when I came back, Erin was on the doorstep. Surprise visit."

Greg smiled. "Thank you, Erin."

"I think her timing was pretty good."

"Did you pack a bag? I planned to drop anchor for the night."

She pulled a small bag from behind her back and grinned. "I'm ready."

He shrugged. "Great. Let's go."

Melanie climbed on board. They untied the boat and Greg took off.

"I'm surprised Emmett trusts me with this thing," he said.

Melanie laughed. "The United States Navy trusts you. I'm not the least bit surprised Emmett does."

"This boat is practically a national treasure. It's Emmett's prized possession."

"He's going to have to get used to being without her. He plans to sell her off."

"Bet he changes his mind," Greg said.

"I don't know. He's got a couple of interested parties."

"I'm not surprised. This boat is special. I wouldn't mind living on her."

Melanie smiled. "We're living on her today, right?"

Greg slowly nodded. Good observation from this beautiful woman.

He examined the way the light shone in her hair and in her eyes. A day and night with Melanie on this boat? Yeah. He planned to enjoy it to the hilt.

**

They spent the day out on the water, enjoying the warm air and sunshine, mist in their faces as Greg let out the sails and picked up speed. He enjoyed the change to have the boat all to himself, without Emmett's instruction. It had been a while since he'd sailed alone, but he'd learned all his life and it all came back quickly.

And he enjoyed Melanie's company.

"Beautiful," Melanie called, shielding her eyes as she looked up at the huge sails.

"They're brand new. Working perfectly."

They enjoyed the sight of other boats in the water, enjoying an afternoon on sailing. Later in the evening, as the sun began to set, they ate the cold sandwiches and fruit Greg had brought.

"I won't eat much," Melanie said.

"Eat as much as you want. I brought a ton." Greg looked over at Melanie while they sat on the deck. "I'm glad you came with me."

She smiled. "Me, too. If Emmett hadn't given me the day off, I was going to find some way to come with you."

"Man, Emmett's tough to work with," Greg said. "I don't know how you deal with him day in, day out."

"I'm used to it. My dad was like that."

"He was?"

She nodded. "A stickler for everything. Never let anything slide. Rules were rules. Didn't get him far, though. He had a heart attack five years ago."

Greg shook his head. "I'm sorry, Mel."

Melanie shrugged. "I lived with nothing but rules and sternness growing up. I didn't like it, but I had to deal with it. And besides, it was all I knew."

He paused for a second. "You deserve better. I don't like you working for him."

"It won't be forever, but for now, it's a job. Don't give it much thought. I'll be fine. And it's just how Emmett is. He'll never change."

"That's for sure." Greg drew in a breath and stared out over the ocean. The boat rocked with an oncoming wave. "You know, I...sometimes think that if I stay in this town, in another ten years I'll look like Emmett."

"He's had a tough life," Melanie said.

"And he's bitter about it."

Melanie nodded.

"He's lived here his whole life, Mel. It's not like he went off to war. He didn't lose everything. His body's intact. His mind's still sharp. He hasn't lost all that much, if you ask me. He doesn't have a good reason to be this bitter."

"He lost his wife."

"She didn't die. She chose to leave him," Greg said.

"I guess you don't blame her."

"Would you stick around for him?" he asked.

Melanie laughed. "I don't know." A grin came over her face. "So you think you'll turn into Emmett if you stay here long enough, huh?"

"I easily could."

"You mean the part about being bitter?"

"Yeah."

"You don't have to turn into Emmett, Greg. You can choose not to be bitter like he has."

"You know why he's like that, right?" Greg asked.

"Everyone knows. He'd talked his whole life about how he wanted to get out of Wyndham Shores. See the world. See everything there is to see. That's why he's so hard on you. Because you've gotten to do those things. He's jealous of you."

Greg stared out at the water. "Guess I hadn't thought about that."

Could be a possibility, though. Rumor had it that at eighteen years old, about to enlist in the Navy, Emmett had gotten his sixteen-year-old girlfriend pregnant. He'd done the right thing by marrying her and raising their baby girl together, but he'd been bitter about it ever since. Then his wife left him for someone else and ran off to see the world while he got stuck behind.

"He's bitter because his wife left him for another guy," Greg said. "After he gave up his whole life for her."

Melanie nodded. "I guess sometimes we regret our choices. Do you know anyone who hasn't?"

Greg shook his head. "He hasn't moved on. I don't think he ever will."

"It's his choice to be the way he is," Melanie said. "He could have chosen something else. Someone else. Instead he spends his time being angry. No one can change that for him."

"I guess not," Greg said.

What was Mel trying to say? That he was headed in that direction if he didn't keep close tabs on the way he acted? Maybe he was headed in that direction.

She lowered her head. "I have something I should tell you. About my own choices I made that weren't great. I was married for a little while."

That shocked him. "You were?"

She nodded. "Sorry I didn't tell you before."

He slowly nodded. "It makes sense that you were married. I mean, I figured somebody would have snapped you up by now. I thought you'd be married by now with a couple of kids."

She drew in a breath. "No. No kids. I wanted them, but…it didn't work out."

"What happened?" he asked. And he had a feeling it was a sore subject.

***

Melanie shifted her weight. For some reason she wanted to tell him the truth about her sordid past. She didn't talk much about her failed marriage, but telling Greg something so intimate drew him closer into her world, and she wanted him closer. She didn't want to keep secrets from him. He'd been through a lot in his own life and maybe he'd understand. Somehow she knew he wouldn't judge her for her choices, or make her feel bad that it didn't work out.

"Was he…anyone I know?" Greg asked.

She shook her head.

"So…it didn't work out," Greg said.

"No. I was twenty and he was twenty-two, and we thought we were in love."

"You weren't."

"We didn't have a clue about anything, much less how to make a life together. We were both trying to figure ourselves out." Melanie sighed. "I think I was looking for someone who loved me, and when he asked if I'd marry him, I jumped at the chance. I thought getting married would solve all of my problems, but it just gave me a whole new set."

"Was he nice to you?" Greg asked.

Melanie shook her head. "The second after we exchanged vows, he showed his true colors. He made me feel guilty for going to school, so I quit, and he made me abandon my friends so I'd have more time to take care of his every need. But nothing I ever did was good enough. He'd come home drunk and angry from work most nights and we fought constantly."

Greg grimaced. "Sounds like a guy with a case of serious self-loathing."

Melanie nodded. "And he took it out on everyone, including me."

"Is that why you divorced?"

"The final straw happened when I got pregnant."

Greg reeled back. Yeah, he wasn't expecting that.

"He hadn't mentioned before we married that he didn't want the responsibility of raising children. I got pregnant by accident, but I'd wanted a family. I'd hoped he'd be happy about it."

"I take it he wasn't."

Melanie looked out at the waves. "He got furious. Told me I should have been more careful. Told me I wrecked his life and our marriage."

"He didn't hit you or anything, did he, Mel?"

Melanie drew in a breath.

Fury shown in Greg's eyes. "I'll kill the guy—"

Melanie put a hand on his chest and smiled. His protective display surprised and pleased her, but it was wasted effort.

"Don't be upset," she said. "He's gone. You don't have to worry about it. He hit me once, and that was it. He disappeared afterward, and if he hadn't, I would have left him. I didn't plan to spend one night in a house with a guy who hit me."

"Good for you for deciding to leave. That was your only option. He wasn't going to change. If he hit you once he would have done it again. No question."

"I know."

Greg looked at her. "So that was it? The guy just left?"

She nodded. "He said he refused to spend the rest of his life working some manual labor job to support a kid."

"So…what happened after that? You have a kid out there—"

She smiled and shook her head. "I would have told you before now if I had."

He nodded.

"I had a miscarriage a month after he'd left. I'd been excited about the prospect of being a single mom and having the baby all to myself, without having to deal with him. I started making all kinds of plans for us. For the first time in my life, I felt focused. I planned to be a good mom."

Greg bit his lip. "You would have been."

"I would have done my best."

"I'm sorry you lost the baby, Mel. That must have been tough."

"It was a tough time. But I guess it wasn't mean to be. And I survived."

"You...you aren't still married, are you?"

She shook her head and smiled. "No." She'd sprung a lot on Greg. Terrified him to death several times in just a few minutes. "I would have told you if I were married. I tracked him down in Florida and filed for divorce. The irony being he was already hooked up with a woman and had already gotten her pregnant."

Greg's eyes widened. "Wow."

"I know. Go figure. I came back here and haven't heard from him. Never will, and that's fine with me."

Melanie had been terrified of getting serious with anyone since, and she had a hard time trusting. But somehow she knew there had to be a guy out there for her. Someone who was different.

She wouldn't tell Greg she'd thought about him during that time and had wondered what it would have been like if they'd had a chance. If he'd chosen her. If he'd so much as looked in her direction and thought…maybe.

"I'm sorry you went through all of that, Mel."

"Thanks. But I guess we all have a story, right? Maybe not a happy one."

"I guess so." Greg pulled her into his arms. "You should finish school, Mel."

"I plan to."

"And don't ever allow someone take your dreams away again, okay?"

"I won't."

Greg kissed her softly. She thought maybe he'd push her away after all she'd revealed, but he didn't seem to be holding it against her.

***

When it grew dark, Greg dropped anchor for the night. He brought out some brownies and cookies from Amelia's coffee shop.

"Sorry I don't have better dessert," he said. "I grabbed the first thing I could find at your friend's coffee shop."

She took a bite of brownie. "This is perfect. Amelia's a great baker."

"I'll take you somewhere for a real dinner and dessert when we get back to shore."

She nodded.

She half-wondered if he'd act strangely toward her after all she'd revealed about herself, but he didn't.

In fact, when he looked at her, she sensed a deeper intimacy there. Like they'd shared some of their deepest secrets and they were both okay with that. It was a good sign, wasn't it?

Melanie felt sticky from being out on the water all day. "Can we take showers?"

"Yeah. We have to, in fact. Emmett wants to make sure the shower works. I just need to make sure I wipe it down good afterward."

"Okay."

Mel showered in the cabin below deck while Greg shut the boat down for the night. She cleaned the sea salt from her body and out of her hair, and came out of the bathroom into the main cabin. She looked at the small bed waiting for them and smiled.

She hadn't brought anything sexy to wear to bed that night. Just a practical shirt and shorts. She brushed her hair out while Greg took a turn in the shower, then sat on the bed and admired the beautiful interior of the cabin.

Greg came out of the shower. She watched him comb his hair and put on underwear and a T-shirt. She watched him moved, his huge arm muscles moving in the soft light. The man was gorgeous and she'd loved watching him work today. Nothing sexier than a strong guy hard at work. It could drive a girl crazy.

He crawled into bed with her. He smelled like soap and shampoo and she could smell his masculine deodorant. "We'll take her back at the first sign of daylight."

She sighed. "It's been a wonderful day."

"Yeah."

She ran her hands through his damp hair and sighed with satisfaction. "You smell good."

"So do you."

Melanie looked around the cabin. "I still can't believe this boat. She's the most beautiful thing I've ever seen."

Greg's gaze locked with Melanie's. "Not me. I'm looking at something much more beautiful. Someone."

Greg leaned in and kissed her. Melanie kissed him back. Just being next to him aroused her, and the feel of his hot mouth on hers turned her on.

"Take off your shirt," he murmured.

She sat and pulled it over her head, but didn't stop there. She unhooked her bra and made no attempt to hide her breasts from him. His eyes grew hazy while he watched her.

Melanie's gaze met his as she climbed off the bed and knelt before him. He sat and moved toward the edge of the bed.

She lifted his shirt and kissed her way down his chest, then planted kisses on him through his boxer briefs, licking him through the soft cotton.

He made her stop while he pulled the boxer briefs off, and his cock strained toward her. She leaned forward and rubbed one of her nipples against it. He adjusted his position, angling his shaft with his hand on the base, holding himself steady while she shifted against him. They both watched the erotic sight of the head of his penis rubbing her tight nipples.

Then she pushed her breasts together and let him side his shaft between them.

"Feel good?" Melanie asked.

He breathed heavily. "Incredible."

Melanie drew away, and then adjusted her position so she could tease his balls with her mouth. She took one sac into her mouth, then the other, alternating between the two until she knew he couldn't take much more.

"Mel."

His hips jerked and she knew what he needed most. His hands threaded through her hair, but she continued to tease his balls gently with her fingers and wouldn't give him what he wanted.

"Mel, suck me," he finally groaned.

She was more than willing to oblige. She took him into her mouth, savoring the taste and texture of him while she sank him to the back of her throat. Her sex pulsed with pleasure while she sucked him in and out, hard, then lightly, then hard again.

She used suction up the length of him and popped him out of her mouth. "Do you like it when I suck you hard?"

"Yes," he panted. "Hard. Fast."

She increased her efforts, stroking in a tight rhythm, and felt him swell to bursting.

"I can't take much more," he groaned. "Pull away. I'm going to—"

She sucked harder. His body jerked with his climax, and hot liquid filled her mouth as he came in a series of hot bursts. He shuddered and groaned when she swallowed.

After a few last strokes of her tongue on the tip and she slowly moved away. His hips involuntarily jerked, like he wasn't ready for her to release him yet. She rested her head in his lap.

"That was unbelievable," he panted.

She listened to the sound of his harsh breathing, her hand resting on his thigh.

"Blowjobs. Great for guys," he said. "Not all that great for women."

"It depends on the guy," she said quietly. "If you like the guy and all... I've always liked giving head, but I'm not all that great at it."

"Are you kidding me? I thought I was going to die with pleasure. Didn't you notice?"

She smiled.

"I love it when you swallow for me," he said on a harsh breath.

She looked up at him. "Did your ex do that for you?"

"Sometimes. She hated it, though. She only did it because she knew I liked it so much."

"I like the taste of it. I like the taste of you. Did she give you oral a lot?"

"Maybe once a month."

He drew her into his lap and slid his hand between her thighs. "You're so wet."

"Yeah. I love sucking you. I almost come when I do it."

"You do?"

She smiled. "Does that surprise you?"

Without answering, Greg pulled her back into the bed with her, a serious look on his face. He brought his mouth to hers, and then kissed his way down her body.

He pulled her shorts and panties off, and when he settled his head between her thighs, Mel drew in a breath.

"You don't have to—"

Greg looked up at her. "I want to, Mel."

Melanie cried out as he kissed one inner thigh, teasing and licking before doing the same thing to the other. She drew in a breath as the tip of his finger slid along the crease of her sex, barely touching her. She'd never been self-conscious about giving, but receiving? Her ex hadn't liked this. Would Greg?

"Greg," she whimpered.

"I want this, Mel. I want to taste you."

She whimpered as he opened her with his fingers. She wanted this badly, so she willed herself to relax.

He slid his tongue along her inner folds, teasing and licking. Then he sank his tongue into her vagina, thrusting in and out, and Melanie's muscles went limp with pleasure. When the tip of his tongue touched her clit she cried out, her hips thrusting up against him.

"Put your hands on my head and show me what you like," he said.

She did what he asked.

She'd always wanted him between her thighs, but the reality of it was more than she could stand. Her hips moved in time with his tongue, pulling him against her, hands buried in his thick dark hair.

He flicked his tongue over her clit again and again, sending her over the edge. Her tremors began and she cried out, holding back her tears. From the pleasure, but also because the one man she'd wanted had given it to her.

When she released her hold on him he eased up and slowly pulled away. She panted and struggled to get air back into her lungs.

"Did your ex do that a lot for you?" he asked.

"Once in a while, when he was drunk."

"Wow.

"He wasn't the most giving guy," she said.

"Doesn't sound like it."

But Greg might not have even wanted to do that for her, either. Just returning the favor. She wondered if she'd ever reach him.

Greg wrapped his arms around her, and she fell into a deep sleep.

***

Greg woke up in the middle of the night. Melanie lay naked in bed beside him. He watched way the moonlight spilled from above and played over the smooth skin of her back. She looked so beautiful and he wanted to touch her soft skin, but he didn't want to wake her.

He went up on deck and drew in deep breaths of sea air in the dark. The night was calm and everything on the boat felt copacetic, so after a few minutes he headed below deck again. Melanie blinked awake and sat in the bed.

He climbed back in beside her and planted lingering kisses over her shoulders. Light, feathery kisses that made her shiver.

"Everything okay with the boat?" she asked.

"Everything's perfect."

"You do good work. Emmett's lucky to have you. He wouldn't have wanted to make this journey himself."

"I'm glad he let us."

"Me, too," she said.

He continued kissing her shoulders. "Lay on your stomach," he whispered.

She rolled over, indulging his request.

He smoothed his hands over her shoulders, savoring the feel of her smooth skin, wanting to lose himself in her. He touched her back, and then ran his hands over the backs of her thighs. He saved the soft flesh of her ass for last. He leaned over and kissed the soft mounds, hands on the curves her hips. His hands slid over her buttocks while he feathered kisses down her back, slowly arousing her. Arousing him.

He stripped off his pants and covered her naked body with his. His hardness slid between her thighs and he slid a finger inside her. She moaned. She was already wet for him.

"That all you want to do?" she asked in a teasing voice.

"Not hardly. Get on your hands and knees, Mel."

He moved back so she could do what he'd asked.

A moment of clarity hit him while he watched her, although he didn't see how clarity was possible when he was hard as a rock. What was he doing, besides taking her from behind in a moment of crazy lust?

"I'm too rough," he ground out.

"No," she said.

"Getting ready to take you like some kind of—"

"I want you to." She breathed hard. "I want you inside me. Now. Like this. Please."

The words excited him. He reached for a condom, hands shaking as he sheathed himself. He tried to be gentle, but pushed through her folds into her soft, willing flesh in one swift stroke. She gasped as he thrust further into her wet heat. He squeezed his eyes shut, savoring the feel of her tight walls contracting around him.

He withdrew to the head but kept it buried inside her. He wanted to pull out all the way and rub the head against her inner lips, teasing her until she cried out with need, but the need to keep contact with her silken heat was too much.

She moved her hips, her little moans of pleasure urging him on. He pulled out and thrust back in again, loving the feel of her channel caressing him, milking him for all he was worth. He moved faster, finding a rhythm. His thrusts became deep as a primitive force took over. He needed to be as deep inside her as he could go when he came.

"Greg, stop," she said, panting. "Wait."

"Am I hurting you?"

"No. Don't move."

Suspended on the brink of pleasure, halfway in and halfway out of her, nothing but the sound of their breathing filling the room, he couldn't think straight.

"Pull out," she said.

"Mel—" He physically couldn't pull his hard cock out when instinct told him to stay in her or die.

"Just do it. It'll be worth it, I promise."

"Mel, come on—"

"You can go in again in a minute."

Everything in him told him to pump into her until he released his seed deep inside her in a burst of hot, white fire. But he did what she asked, groaning while he pulled his cock from her wet heat. Cool air blew over his turgid shaft.

Their pants filled the room. She was right. His pleasure grew.

"Come on, Mel," he said roughly.

"Just wait." She breathed hard. "You can touch my back with your hands. I liked that. Nothing else."

He smoothed his hands over the soft skin of her back, and then reached for her behind. She had the most perfect ass he'd ever seen, and he smoothed his hands over the soft skin. Perfect. She was driving him mad. He slid his fingers between her legs to the soft pink inner lips. He grazed her with the tip of his finger, and she shivered.

His cock jerked and his balls ached, begging for release. He could wait no longer, and positioned himself at her entrance, sliding against her slick fresh. "I need to be in you again," he growled.

She breathed hard. "Yes. Now."

He entered her again in one hard thrust and pumped into her for all he was worth. Hard. Hot. Their cries filled the room as he brought them both to the brink.

"Yes," she whimpered. "Harder."

He obliged, pumping in a tight rhythm.

"Almost there." She gasped. "Don't stop."

He felt his climax building in his balls but held off. Then her inner walls began gripping his cock in a series of hard spasms, and he could hold back no longer. He shouted out his pleasure as burst after burst of hot liquid spurted forth, and he wanted nothing more than his semen flooding deep inside her vagina instead of the latex sheath. He mourned that even as his climax consumed him. One day, he thought. One day he'd come inside her bare, flooding her with nothing between them.

His lungs burned, and he gasped for air. He'd ever come so hard in his entire life.

He felt her tremors as she gasped and cried out and moved her hips against him. Then she slowed down, gasping for breath.

He slowly withdrew, her channel tightening around him as he pulled out inch by inch. Sheer torture.

Greg rolled onto his back and gathered her up in his arms.

It terrified him. He cared about her. Could even love her. He'd vowed not to get mixed up in this. Never to fall in love again. He didn't deserve love. Didn't deserve the pleasure Melanie gave him. Didn't deserve to have a woman who'd given herself to him without reservations the way Melanie had.

He would leave Wyndham Shores soon, and he wasn't ready to start over with Melanie. He didn't want a serious relationship again. He'd ruined it before, and that part of his life was over.

Maybe this romantic adventure hadn't been such a great idea. It made him want things he could no longer have.

Chapter Four

Greg woke up in sheer heaven. He couldn't remember falling asleep last night, but right now he was having the best dream he'd ever had. He never wanted to wake up from it. Pleasure flowed through his body and he felt like he was on fire in the best way—

His eyes popped open to the most beautiful sight: Melanie naked and leaning over him, her hand on his cock. This was no dream. He tried to sit but all he could do was fall back onto the pillow.

He sucked in a breath. Hell of a way to wake him up.

She touched him softly, her fingertips lightly tracing the head. He settled beneath her, watching her as she wrapped her hand gently around his shaft and began to stroke.

A hand job. He groaned out his surprise, his thighs quaking. He hadn't had a hand job in forever and had forgotten how exciting it could be.

She teased him with light strokes and it drove him crazy. He thrust his hips up, making it clear he needed her to work him harder, faster. She didn't. He wanted to put his hand over hers and show her what he liked, but held back. He shut his eyes tight and savored the slow build toward orgasm.

Then suddenly she gripped his shaft and pumped hard. He shuddered and thrust into her hand while she worked her magic, loving the pleasure she gave him. He stiffened, preparing to come in her hand. But then she eased up on the pressure of her strokes. So close to getting the release he craved, his eyes flew open in protest.

She looked up at him with a mischievous look in her eyes, then leaned down and replaced her hand with her mouth in one smooth move. He could hardly believe what he just saw...what he felt. Her taking his cock deeply into her mouth. He'd died and gone to heaven. He wanted to make this last, but he was too far gone. Two thrusts of her mouth and the orgasm hit like a freight train. He burst into her, over and over, an explosion of pleasure.

She gave him a few last lingering licks, then looked up at him and smiled. "Bait and switch."

He managed to smile back at her between harsh gasps. In another week he might be able to breathe.

"You're killing me, Mel."

"That's the idea."

"Quite a wakeup call you just gave me."

"That reminds me. Good morning."

He laughed. "Good morning."

She lay down beside him, her head resting on his shoulder. "I figured I should wake you up so we can get moving."

"Yeah. Good idea. But we've got a few minutes."

"To play around?" she teased.

"Yeah."

He took her breasts in his hands, palming them. Then he kissed his way down her stomach and cupped her mound with one hand. He parted her thighs and feathered kisses over her soft skin. Then he planted soft kisses down the crease between her thighs.

"Please, Greg. I'm going to faint." She looked like she was about to cry, and he was bordering on cruelty.

It wasn't right to torture her. She cried out, and then he could take no more. He opened her with his fingers, the heavenly scent of her sex driving him crazy. She whimpered when he licked over her folds, over and over, the liquid heat of her like honey on his tongue. Then he sank his tongue into her, sliding in and out until she cried out and grabbed his head. She ran her fingers through his hair and pulled him closer.

He turned his attention to her sensitive nub, kissing her as gently as he could and then making little wisps of his tongue against her. Her hips thrust up against his mouth in a frantic rhythm.

He felt the hot rush of her release and bent his head to taste her ecstasy.

"Greg," she whimpered.

He needed to bury himself inside her and surround himself with her heat, but he knew how sensitive she'd be after her climax. He'd given her that release, and it filled him with arrogant satisfaction. That would be enough for now.

***

When they got back to the dock, they washed the sheets and towels and dishes, leaving the boat cleaner than when they'd taken her out.

Melanie gave Greg a mischievous grin while she put the sheets back on the bed. "I wonder what Emmett would think of our activities on the boat."

"He's never going to find out."

Melanie laughed. "I know. He'd die."

Greg grinned. "We'll let him think we played Checkers the whole time."

Melanie laughed again. They'd had incredible sex, and Melanie could hardly believe it. A little spark went off in her brain as she recalled what Amelia had said about getting hurt. Melanie couldn't help wondering if this really was just sex, or if Greg actually felt something for her.

She definitely felt for Greg. She didn't know how she'd let him go, and even though they hadn't been together long, it would take her forever to get over him.

Emmett showed up on the dock an hour later, just as they finished cleaning up.

"Emmett, what are you doing here?" Melanie asked. "You should be home in bed."

"I spent all day yesterday resting. I'm fine." He turned to Greg. "How'd she do?"

"She was perfect," Greg replied.

"I want that report. In detail."

"I've got the checklist and I made a log of the whole trip. It's below deck. I'll get it," Greg said.

"Did she have any trouble on any part of it? Anything at all I need to know about."

"It's all in the report, but no. It went great."

Greg went below deck and came back up with the report. He handed it to Emmett. "How's that cold?"

"Doesn't matter." Emmett coughed and took the report. "I just need to know how much work we have left on her."

"Not that much. She's in great shape."

Emmett examined the report for a minute and then squinted up at Greg. "Nice work."

"Thanks."

Emmett looked at the report again and nodded his approval. As the old guy walked off without any further questions, Greg looked at Melanie and winked.

She grinned at him. They'd gotten away with it. What happened between them on the boat would be their little secret, and she'd never forget it.

***

That night, Greg took Melanie to Marco's, a little hole-in-the-wall Italian place near the docks. The wooden shack with shabby red leather booths wasn't much to look at, inside or out, but the food was incredible.

They shared a pizza and a garden salad, and afterward as they walked back through the main drag of town, arm-in-arm toward Greg's truck, Melanie stopped in her tracks.

"Great." She stared straight ahead and pulled Greg closer. "Shawn."

Shawn had been stuffing his face with a calzone when they'd come inside the restaurant. She and Greg had picked a table for two off to the side and out of the way, minding their own business, but Melanie had still caught Shawn staring at them all through dinner. He'd finished eating and walked out long before they had, and she'd hoped he'd gone home. Now she knew he hadn't been able to resist coming back for a confrontation.

"Where you going, fly boy?" Shawn asked.

"Home," Greg said.

If anything was wrong no one would know it from the calm expression on Greg's face.

"Wyndham Shores isn't home for you anymore," Shawn said. "Aren't you in the Army or something?"

"Or something."

Shawn shoved Greg. "Then what are you doing back here?"

"Stop it," Melanie said.

Greg made no move to hit him back. Shawn punched Greg in the gut as hard as he could, and Greg stood there taking it.

"Shawn, get out of here," Melanie cried.

"No way." Shawn stared intently at Greg. "You got a lot of nerve showing your face around here."

Greg breathed hard from his punch but stood strong. "I won't hit you, Shawn. But I will ask you to get the hell out of here."

"Shawn—" Melanie said.

"It's all right, Mel," Greg said.

"Shut up, man," Shawn whined. "You're not fit to speak to her. You're garbage." He turned to Melanie. "Why are you with him, Mel? You deserve better."

Melanie moved closer and put her hand on Greg's bicep, making it clear he belonged to her and vice versa.

"You deserve someone better," Shawn said.

"I've got the best man I've ever known," she asked.

"Best man, my ass. A cheating asshole, more like it. He'll cheat on you, too, Mel. That's what he does. He screws everyone he can without a thought for anyone but himself. He tears families apart and ruins lives. You could have a guy like me, who wouldn't—"

"Go, Shawn." Melanie's eyes filling with tears. "Live your own life."

Shawn pointed a shaking finger at Greg. "Leave town, fly boy. Don't come back."

"Go home, Shawn. You're drunk," Greg said. "Just go on home."

Shawn backed away.

Melanie turned to Greg. "Did he hurt you?"

"No."

"He socked you in the gut."

"I can handle it."

Melanie watched Shawn limp off. The guy acted like he'd been the one punched in the gut. Rage filled her at the fact that he'd hurt Greg.

"Why didn't you beat the crap out of him?" she asked.

"I can't hit some drunken guy, Mel."

"But he's…he scarred up your face last time, Greg."

"He's all talk. If he'd gone for my face I would have done something, and it wouldn't have been pretty."

She shook her head. "I'd love to see you beat that guy senseless."

"No, you wouldn't, Mel," he said darkly.

She rested her head on his arm. "I'll never stand by and watch you get hurt. Ever."

Greg put his arm around her, holding her close. "You won't have to." He leaned down and planted a kiss in her hair. "Come on. Let's go."

They walked along the water, and Mel wrapped her arm around Greg's waist, letting her hand rest on his ass.

"He's such a jerk," she said.

"Yeah. But maybe he's right about one thing."

Greg quit walking and the air around them went silent. Almost everyone had gone home for the night and the only sound was the gentle lapping of waves against the boats.

Melanie shook her head. "You didn't tear that family apart, Greg—"

"Maybe I'm not good enough for you, Mel."

She furrowed her brow. "Don't say that. Why would you say that?"

"Because maybe he's right. You deserve better."

Greg released his hold on her and paced in front of her. "Nothing can change the fact that I cheated, with the worst possible person I could have cheated with."

"You made a mistake. One night shouldn't be the judge of a person," Melanie said. "One night shouldn't have ruined your whole life."

"One night can definitely ruin someone's life." His humorless laugh echoed into the night. "Hell, one minute can ruin someone's life. One second. No question one night can change everything."

Melanie bit her lip. "I'll bet you've never told anyone exactly what happened and why you did it."

Greg grimaced and shook his head. "Nobody wants to know the details. They're irrelevant."

"Tell me. I want to know," she said.

He ran hand through his hair. "How I ended up cheating on my wife with her sister?"

Melanie nodded. "I know you loved Maxine. I have a feeling something bad happened between you two. Like a knock-down, drag out fight. Am I right?"

Greg quit pacing and lowered his head.

"You don't have to answer," she said. "I just wondered. It's a mystery. Everyone's filled in the blanks on their own, but I think they're wrong. There are two sides to every story."

"No one's ever asked for my side."

"I'm asking," she said.

Greg drew in a deep breath as they slowly started walking again. "You're right. Maxine and I had a knock-down, drag out fight one night. She used to spend more time than I liked talking to Allen on her cell. She worked with this guy, but I didn't see why they had to go for coffee together every single day. One time she invited him to a party at work while I was home on leave. She said she thought I'd be at sea that week and she'd already invited him. She didn't want to go alone. I only had two days of leave to spend with her and I didn't want her going with Allen, so I got angry. So did she. She kicked me out for the night."

He blew out a deep breath. "I accused her of wanting to have an affair with Allen, which really pissed her off. She called me a jealous asshole and said she hated me, and that she never wanted to see me again. She ended up going with Allen to the party that night."

Melanie blinked. "What did you do?"

A shamed look came over his face. "I was so furious I went to Luddy's Tavern to get drunk. Erika was there. It was her twenty-first birthday and she was...let's just say she was ready for some action with someone. Maybe it didn't even matter who. I knew it wasn't right but that night I didn't care."

"She'd been interested in you for a while, hadn't she?" Melanie asked.

Greg shrugged. "Maybe so."

"I know she was." Melanie's gaze met his. "I know she used to hit on you every chance she got. I think she had a major thing for you, but I also think she saw a chance to hurt her big sister that night and she took it."

Greg drew in a deep breath. "Maybe so. I was a conquest. The whole time I was with her, I knew it was wrong. Anyway, the next day I came home and Maxine let me back into the house, ready to forgive me. She thought I'd spent the night at the motel. Then Erika showed up and told Maxine I'd slept with her and that we were running away together. Maxine lost it. She told me I'd just ruined our marriage. I told Maxine it was a one-time deal, and I begged her to forgive me."

"What did she say?"

"She told me she'd never forgive me for hurting her." His voice cracked. "She said I'd ruined our marriage and nothing would ever be the same."

"Greg, when you slept with Erika, you were hurt—"

"It doesn't matter. It wasn't right, Mel." He hung his head in shame. "There's no excuse for cheating on her with her sister because I was angry and jealous."

"You won't do it again. I know you won't."

He lowered his head and slowly shook it. "I should have thought of that before. And now it's too late. I can't take it back."

Melanie swallowed the lump in her throat. "Greg, you can't torture yourself over this for the rest of your life. It's time you let it go. You can choose to move on. You can choose to forgive yourself."

"I can't."

"Erika is okay. Maxine is okay. You're the only one suffering right now."

"Yeah, well…maybe I deserve it."

She moved closer to him and leaned her head on his shoulder. "I'm glad you got that off your chest. I think you've needed to tell someone your side of the story for a long time."

"Yeah, I guess I have."

"I—"

Greg brought his mouth to hers and cut her off with a kiss. She blinked when he pulled back.

"I don't want to talk about the past anymore," he said.

"We don't have to."

Greg brushed a lock of hair behind her ear, and she saw the first signs of a smile break out over his face. "I didn't know Shawn had a thing for you."

Melanie shrugged. "I've never been interested in him."

"I never thought he'd be jealous of me, but when he saw me with you…I don't blame him for being jealous. If the roles were reversed, and you were with him, I'd be jealous of him."

"You would?" she asked.

He nodded. "He wants you. And I'd never want you with a guy like him."

"Yeah? Well, you never have to worry about that, trust me. I want you."

***

When they got back to Greg's house, he collapsed on the couch. "You did want to stay here, right? Should I take you home?"

Melanie shook her head. "I don't want to go home. Does your stomach hurt from that punch?"

He shook his head.

"Good." She waggled her brows at him. "Because I had big plans for us tonight."

He laughed. "As much as I want you, I think my performance would be sup-par tonight."

"You tired?"

He nodded.

She clasped her hands behind her back and shrugged. "I could do all the work."

He laughed. "A very generous offer. But do you still want me, Mel? After what I told you?"

She nodded. "I still want you," she said softly.

She dragged him to his feet and pressed her lips gently against his. After a minute of barely grazing his lips with her tongue, Greg became more than an eager participant, kissing her back hungrily. The desire in his kisses turned her on, and all Mel wanted was to make love to him.

She learned something new about him each minute they spent together, and her love for him grew. She loved how protective he'd been, how he always back out of the situation without using force. He had the power to hurt someone but chose not to. He chose to do the right thing, and it turned her on. She wondered if she'd be strong enough to turn the other way if someone treated her the way Shawn treated Greg.

When they got in the bedroom Mel pulled off her panties.

"Take off your clothes and get on the bed," she said.

He grinned at the orders she'd given. "Yes, ma'am."

He did what she asked without hesitation. She straddled him on the bed and his hands went to her hips.

Mischief twinkled in his eyes. "I like it when you boss me around."

She laughed. "You do?"

"Yeah. It's hot."

"Oh, really."

He was already hard and she wanted to do this with no foreplay. Just get straight to it. She lightly touched his shaft with her fingers, watching him stiffen and grow until he was hard enough for her to slide on a condom.

Then she lifted her dress and positioned him at her entrance. She rubbed herself on him, letting the head open her flesh, stretching her. She gasped as he breached her entrance. She moved downward, a little at a time, and then worked away on top of him, moving her hips in circles, then back. She enjoyed taking him all the way in, then out to the head, all the way in again, and back up, squeezing his shaft all the while. Then she bounced on top of him. He watched from underneath her.

"Take off the dress." He breathed hard.

She stopped moving and pulled it over her head.

His gaze roamed over her belly, then her breasts. "Now the bra."

He watched with hazy eyes while she unhooked her bra and tossed it aside. Her nipples went rock hard as his hands cupped her breasts.

He gently twisted her nipples with his fingers and delicious sensations flowed through her down to her core. She moaned, the moisture between her thighs easing the friction as she moved on top of him again.

"Squeeze me tight inside you," he said.

She squeezed her inner muscles around his shaft.

"Yes." He squeezed his eyes shut. She relaxed, and then slid him in and out a few times. Then she squeezed again. "Tighter," he said.

She squeezed for all she was worth, and he watched her, a look of ecstasy on his face. They stayed like that, her squeezing around him, letting go, and squeezing him tight again. She reached behind her and fingered his balls, and felt a jolt go through him. He pumped into her while she moved above him and tried to meet him thrust for thrust.

After a few minutes he put his hands on her hips, slowing her down. "Mel, let's change this up some."

She stopped, resting for a second. "You're not tired anymore?"

"I've got my energy back."

She laughed. "So I see."

She rolled onto her back and savored the feel of Greg thrusting inside her, slowly, deliberately, drawing out each thrust until they both gasped. He quickened, and then slowed again. She shifted her hips, needing him in deep. She wanted this to last as long as he could hold out.

"Stay there," she said. "Don't move."

Greg pushed deeper inside and stayed there. The head bumped her cervix and she shifted her hips.

"I love you," Melanie whispered.

She'd said the words she should have waited to hear from him. But then again, why hide the truth? She loved him and needed to say it. It hadn't been all that much of a risk, had it? Saying those words during sex didn't count. He wouldn't remember later.

"I need to move," he said.

"Yes," she panted.

He began to move again, faster which each thrust. Then he paused for a second, and she felt him swell within her. He was close to coming. So was she.

Melanie lost herself in a moment of fantasy. She wished they could go away somewhere and live happily ever after. Escape this town and everyone in it and never come back. Start over together, where no one would give them disapproving looks in restaurants. She could be with him and never, ever have to date another loser who didn't care about her.

But she knew happily ever after didn't exist other than in fairy tales. Greg hadn't said I love you back. Not even now, during sex. Was there anything she could do to make him love her?

Greg suddenly pulled out of her. "Get at the edge of the bed."

She did what he asked. He adjusted himself, feet flat on the floor, and she opened her thighs wide. He entered her again and began a quick rhythm in and out, pumping into her for all he was worth. She pressed her finger against her clit, moving in time with his thrusts.

He groaned. "You feel so good, Mel. You're so tight. So wet. It feels incredible."

She moaned out something unintelligible. Could no longer form words. The pleasure was almost unbearable as he brought her toward the most unbelievable orgasm of her life. Greg looked down at himself thrusting in and out of her. She knew the view of them together like this turned him on. She lifted her head, sharing the erotic sight of their bodies joining.

Her tremors began, and she gave in to the earth-shattering orgasm. Seconds later he shouted out his own climax.

Greg collapsed and crawled into the bed with her. He rolled onto his back beside her, breathing hard. "Man, you're great in bed, Mel."

She touched his shoulder. "Only with you. Just because of how I feel about you."

"I thought I'd go insane on the boat. And to-night."

"Me, too."

Melanie snuggled up against him. She wanted to be something more to him than just great in bed. It made her weak to care about him and expect him to care about her in return. Yes, they'd had amazing sex, but she wondered if it went beyond that. The sex couldn't be this good unless he felt something for her, could it?

Greg held her, but didn't say anything else. He didn't tell her he loved her. Maybe she didn't meant anything to him, and she'd been kidding herself all this time to think she had.

She wasn't ashamed to admit to herself she wanted so much more than sex. But could she admit it to him?

She had to tell him how she felt, or risk him leaving, and she'd never know the rest of her whole life what would have happened if she'd said something.

It was a big risk, but time was running out. He would be leaving soon, and it would be a risk she'd have to take.

***

The next afternoon, Craig helped Greg move equipment on the dock of Lady Luck. The sun shone brightly and Greg had worked hard, trying to finish up the last of the work that needed to be done. The boat couldn't be in better shape.

Craig wiped sweat from his brow. "I got a call yesterday. A couple of guys turned in their wings. They'll need us back sooner than we thought."

"You sure?" Greg asked.

"We'll probably get the calls later today."

"How much longer do you think we have?" Greg asked.

"A few more days. A week, max."

Greg nodded.

Damn. He needed more than that to figure out what was happening with him and Melanie. They'd had a great time together, but was he ready for some kind of commitment? He scrubbed a hand over his face. He didn't think he could go there again. He wasn't ready for a relationship or anything else. But could he leave her without a word? What would he say to her?

She'd told him she loved him last night. What the hell did that mean?

Was his leave getting cut short a sign that he needed to move on? That they both did? That she needed to finish school? Maybe he'd come here to make her realize she needed to finish school and get out from under Emmett's thumb. School would give her something real, and love would only cause her pain.

Damn. Hadn't she had enough pain? Had love ever caused her anything but?

Whether they'd both said this would be nothing more than sexual healing, he still felt like an ass. She deserved better.

He knew deep down they'd gone beyond sexual healing, and it threw him into a panic.

**

Amelia served Melanie a cup of coffee early the next morning. "I heard Greg's leaving," Amelia said.

Bleary eyed before six o'clock and not sure she'd heard her correctly, Melanie blinked. "Where'd you hear that?"

"He told Emmett yesterday afternoon."

"Could be a rumor."

Amelia nodded. "He told Emmett he got called away. The Navy needs him. They're shipping him out to sea again. He'll be gone for three months."

Melanie hadn't heard from him the night before. She'd wondered if he'd been avoiding her for some reason, and deep down she knew what Amelia was saying was true. "Where'd you hear this?"

"Craig's already been in to get coffee this morning. He's leaving, too." Amelia examined her face. "Oh, no. You didn't know, did you?"

Melanie bit her lip, tears forming in her eyes. She had to find out if this was true or not. "I'll see you later." She rushed out the door.

"Mel!" Amelia called. "Wait!"

Melanie let the door shut behind her. Greg was leaving, and he wasn't even going to say goodbye.

Chapter Five

The sun shone brightly as Melanie rushed out to the dock, and sweat broke out on her brow. It was stupid of her to rush after him, but she could not, and would not let him go without telling her goodbye. It wasn't right that everyone else knew he was leaving before she did. After everything that happened, he at least owed her a goodbye. Her heart had been ripped from her chest at the thought that he hadn't even done that for her.

He didn't even want to give them a chance. He didn't want to try, or ask her if she wanted to try.

Greg was hard at work on the boat. Luckily, Emmett was nowhere in sight and neither was anyone else. Good. She needed this to be a private conversation.

"I missed you last night." She folded her arms across her chest.

"I, uh…guess I needed an evening to myself. To think things through."

She nodded. "I figured. I heard you're leaving."

He squinted up at her.

"Everyone in town knows but me." She bit her lip and tears filled her eyes. Hold off. Don't let him see you cry.

"I'm sorry about that, Mel. Rumors spread fast."

"But it's not a rumor. It's true. Isn't it?"

He grimaced and then nodded, and a fresh wave of pain crashed through her.

"You weren't going to tell me?" she asked.

"I was going to tell you. I just didn't know how."

Her gaze narrowed. She couldn't believe this. Couldn't believe how cold the idea of him leaving was. A chill went through her. How could he stand here looking at her when he'd been so cold?

"Were you even going to say goodbye to me?" she asked.

"I was, Mel."

She bit her lip. "So that's it. Goodbye. Thanks for the memories."

"Mel—"

She drew in a breath. "What now? You leave and we never see each other again?"

"I don't know when I'm coming back. I'm sorry. It's my job. I have to do this."

"Alone."

"Yes. I've always had to do this alone."

"You haven't always been alone. You've had people who cared about you. Then you had Maxine. You weren't so alone when you were with her."

"I felt alone a lot of the time I was with Maxine. Just because we were married didn't mean we always connected. Didn't mean we were always on the same page."

"But you supported one another emotionally. Didn't you?"

"No. Not always," he said quietly.

"Do you even think it's possible for two people to connect?" she asked.

Greg shook his head. "I'm not sure, Mel. I've never experienced it."

"You don't think we connected? On any level?"

He lowered his head and shook it. "I'll let you down, Mel. Maybe not next week or next month, but sooner or later, I'll let you down and we'll both be hurt."

Her heart sank. "What is wrong with you, Greg?"

"I've asked myself that question a thousand times."

"What are you so afraid of?"

"What do you want from me? I'm leaving. You knew I was leaving. We're both better off this way. I can't do anything about this. When I get called—"

She held her head high. "You could ask me to come with you."

"I can't do that." He stared at the ground and shook his head again. "You're angry. It always ends up like this. With anyone I get close to being angry with me."

"At least you admitted you got close to me."

He went silent.

"Didn't you?" she asked. "Is that what you're admitting?"

Greg didn't answer, and her frustration raged.

"Is it that hard to admit we got close? That maybe what happened between us was more than sex?"

"I don't know, Mel."

"Wow." She gave a humorless laugh. "You're ice cold with me, Greg. I mean nothing to you."

"I told you the first night we were…together…that I had nothing to offer you. I want to be able to give you more, but I can't. I've got nothing to give. You saw how I screwed things up with me and Maxine. I destroyed my marriage and I almost destroyed myself. You and I are both better off if I go off alone."

"That's an excuse. A sorry excuse. You have a lot to give, and I don't want you going off alone."

"Then what do you want?"

"I want you to give us a chance."

He shook his head. "You don't want me, Mel."

"I do want you. I've always wanted you, and it's caused me nothing but pain. I shouldn't want you, but I have, since we were kids. Since the day that day in high school when you stood up for someone getting bullied, I knew what kind of man you were and I loved you for it. You never even knew who I was, much less cared. I don't know why I thought you'd notice me. I don't know why I thought I could make you see me. That I could make you see how good we'd be together. You still don't see it, after everything that's happened. I've been the biggest fool I can possibly imagine all this time."

"You're the most giving woman I've ever met in my life. You deserve someone who can give you that and more."

"A giving woman," she said, bitterness in her voice. "Sure. A lot of good it's done me."

"You'll be a nurse. If that's what you want, go after it."

"I will. I was hoping I could go after it with you. That I'd have your support behind me."

"You do have my support. I just won't be in the same city."

"Great."

"I know you can do it alone. You don't need me."

"I know I can do it alone," she said. "But I wanted to do it with someone I love."

Melanie shook her head. How could she tell him what was in her heart? Tears formed in her eyes but she pushed them back. Why should she wear her heart on her sleeve when he had no feelings for her in return? Why should she put herself out there and tell him how she felt when he couldn't do the same for her?

"Maxine will run your life forever. You'll never let go of what happened with her. You'll never forgive yourself for cheating on her, and you'll never let yourself move on."

"Aren't you afraid I'll cheat on you, Mel?"

"After the grief you've put yourself though?" She scoffed. "Not a chance. Out of all the men I've ever met, I'd put my bet on you to be the most faithful man in the world. Despite what happened, you were a faithful man."

"No. I wasn't."

"You slipped up once, and you've paid your price. You've done your penance and you need to forgive yourself for what you've done," Melanie said.

Greg couldn't look at her. He couldn't even gather up the decency to look at her and it burned through her. "I'm sorry, Mel."

She grunted. "Huh. You're sorry. You've paid the price and suffered every day. She's moved on, and you're on your own. She's happy with her man and her life, and it's like you won't even let yourself be happy. She's not watching anymore. You're free."

Melanie drew in a breath. "Your wife didn't even deserve you. And she's all you can think about. Your mistake is all you can think about. I always believed you deserved a second chance to be happy. But it's not with me, is it."

Greg didn't answer.

Then Melanie got it. A light bulb went off in her brain and the clouds cleared away, leaving her with nothing but blue sky and clarity. Even if he forgave himself and decided to move on, he still wouldn't want to be with her.

"There's something bigger here," she said quietly. "I can't believe I didn't see this before. It was here all the time, right in front of me. You don't love me."

She wanted to fall to the ground and scream and cry. She wanted to reclaim all the time she'd wasted vying for his attention and his love, but she couldn't.

"You don't love me and you never will," she said.

Nothing she did or said would ever change that.

"I can't love you, Mel, and you deserve someone who can. You deserve to finish school. You deserve your dreams."

Melanie looked at him with disbelief.

"I want you to be happy," he said. "You're better off without me."

"Right."

Greg gave her a kiss on the mouth, but she wasn't into it and refused to kiss him back. She wanted a hell of a lot more than a kiss goodbye, and she'd never get it.

She tore herself away from him. "Do me a favor and leave without saying goodbye, just like you'd planned. I don't even want your goodbye anymore."

Head lowered, a hurt look on his face, Greg got back to work.

As she walked back off the dock, Melanie didn't even have the strength to cry.

***

Greg had a beer with Craig in Luddy's Tavern that night.

"Emmett took a bid," Craig said. "The buyer's coming for the boat tomorrow."

"That's good," Greg said.

"Bought and paid for. Apparently the guy paid a fortune for Lady. More than what Emmett asked. He wants to give you a share for all of your hard work."

"He can keep it. I'll take money for the work I did and that's all. Tell him to share the profits with Melanie."

"You earned it."

"I'd rather she have it."

"Fine with him, I'm sure." Craig chuckled and took a swig of beer. "He never liked you, anyway."

Greg gave a half-smile. "I know."

"I think the guy's sad to let the boat go," Craig said. "It's been his pride and joy, working on that thing."

"Yeah, it was. But he'll find another boat to restore, and he'll sell that one, too. It's what he does."

Craig smirked. "You would know what that's like, right?"

Greg furrowed his brow. "What are you saying?"

"Just that you're the king of emotional un-attachment."

"Who says I'm the king of——?"

"Me. I saw you with Melanie this afternoon. I came in at the end of your fight."

Greg shook his head. "I wish you'd minded your own business."

"She looks at you like a woman in love, and you've hurt her. I could see it all over her face."

"I never meant to hurt her," Greg said darkly. "She's better off without me. She just doesn't know it yet."

Craig chuckled again. "Wow. Are you a coward or what?"

"I've been called worse."

"So that's it? You're going to walk away from her? No strings attached?"

"We were together only for a few weeks. We both knew that."

It sounded harsh. Cold. Yeah, he was all of those things and worse.

"Off on your own again, huh? You're not plan-ning to try to make it work with her? Ask her to come with you?"

"She belongs here."

"What are you so afraid of?"

"Nothing. I'm not afraid of anything."

Craig shook his head.

"What's the matter?"

"I think you're full of shit," Craig said.

"It's for the best."

"Right. Do you want to be alone?" Craig asked. "Because that's where you're headed, my friend. A lifetime of being alone. You might see yourself being a decorated Navy Captain in your future, and maybe you think that'll make you happy. Maybe that will be enough for you. But all I see is a future crotchety old man, bitter because life didn't work out the way he wanted."

"Thanks a lot."

"It's the truth. I see a guy who could have made other choices, but decided to throw away his chance for a good life."

Was that true? Would Greg turn into Emmett?

"You've got a woman who's loved you since the dawn of time," Craig said.

"What are you talking about?"

"Come on, man. It's no secret Melanie Grantham has always been in love with you. Everyone in town knows. I think you know it, too, only you've always treated her like dirt—"

"That's not true."

"You've ignored her until now. And something finally happens between the two of you. The timing was right. You're both in a good place to start over with someone new, and you've got a chance for a future with her. So what, you're going to throw it away?" Craig shook his head. "Man, I wouldn't treat anybody like that. You take it for granted. If I had a woman like that who loved me…"

"You'd what?"

A huge smile came over Craig's face. "I'd take her away somewhere and live happily ever after."

Greg shook his head and said darkly, "There's no such thing."

"Then I'd die trying for it."

***

Melanie had a quiet dinner with Amelia in a tiny restaurant that evening. She needed a change of scenery. She'd finally gotten her car out of the shop and relished the drive along the ocean alone.

After they ate they walked along the boardwalk. A cool breeze blew. It reminded Melanie that fall would be coming soon, and she looked forward to it. It would be her last fall in Wyndham Shores, and she'd enjoy every second of it before she left. But the time had come for her to go.

"I'm sorry it didn't work out with Greg," Amelia said.

Melanie tried to smile. "I'm fine." She drew in a breath of salty air. "Okay. I'm not okay. But I will be. I'm going to be making some changes in my life."

Amelia furrowed her brow. "Like what?"

"I'm going to put myself a little further up the list from now on. Be more proactive about going after my dreams."

"That's a good."

"I'll get my A.D.N. in December. I never thought I'd go for it, but I want my bachelor's degree. I'll start looking at schools and filling out applications now. I'd like to start classes in the spring."

"Would you move somewhere?"

"There's a small college outside Boston I want to go check out tomorrow. I want that degree, and I know now I need to get out of Wyndham Shores."

"Will you come back here after you finish school?"

Melanie shook her head. "I think it's time I saw something else. Went somewhere different. I could get a job at a hospital in the big city."

"Wow." Amelia shook her head. "That sounds…ambitious."

Melanie smiled. "About time I got some ambition in me."

"I'm happy for you, Mel, but I don't want to lose you."

"Wherever I am you can come visit me."

Amelia grinned. "That would be great. I never get to go anywhere with the shop and all. But aren't you scared?"

Melanie drew in a deep breath. "Yes, but I'm going to do it anyway. It's time. I can't wait around and watch everyone else's life go on while mine stays in neutral. Besides, I don't want to still be hanging around here next time Greg rolls through town. If he ever comes through again."

"I hate that he broke your heart. I knew he'd get all the sex he wanted and then say Sayonara, sweetheart. I knew it! I tried to warn you that a guy like him—"

"Amelia—"

"You deserve more," Amelia said. "You deserve so much more than a guy who couldn't care less about you. And who used you for sex."

"He wasn't using me any more than I used him."

"Ha. You didn't use him. You've always cared for him." Amelia gave her a disapproving look. "You gave him more than he deserved in bed, I'm sure." She scoffed. "Giving yourself to him body and soul without asking for anything in return. Of course it was a recipe for disaster."

How could Melanie deny she'd given herself to him body and soul? And he hadn't wanted her.

"That was my choice. And I never thought about what I could get in return. It wasn't about that," Melanie said softly.

"Wake up, Mel. You deserve a man who gives back what you give. You deserve someone who loves you as much as you love him, and it's not Greg. You're always an optimist, and I love that about you. It's one of your best qualities, but it's also your downfall. You always see the good in people, and you always think they'll come around. Sometimes they do. But Greg won't come around, and I don't want you wasting one minute of your precious life thinking he will."

Melanie blinked as the words sank in. She knew Amelia was right, and the truth hurt.

She loved Greg. She'd seen her future with him. In some strange way, her heart belonged to him and she would always love him, no matter who they ended up with, or if they ended up alone. But Amelia had a point. As agonizing and against her nature as it might be, she needed to put aside her romantic notions and face reality.

"You want to be with someone who loves you as much as you love him, don't you?" Amelia asked.

"Yes."

"Maybe he's not capable of that. Wouldn't it break your heart to be with a man like that, day in and day out?"

Melanie nodded. It would.

Did she want to go through life watching other couples in love and knowing she'd never have that? What good was having the man of her dreams if he didn't love her back every bit as much? How long could she pretend that Greg would come around?

Tears filled her eyes. She couldn't make him forgive himself for what he'd done any more than she could make him love her.

"I can't believe I spent so much of my life in love with a guy who didn't want me," Melanie said. "I hate myself for being so foolish. For giving myself to someone who didn't want me."

"If you leave, at least I won't have to stand by and watch you be with someone who uses you. Greg doesn't even deserve you. I'm glad you're moving on and going after your dreams. Live your life and forget about him."

Melanie nodded.

At least now she knew she'd never settle for anything less than a man who cared about her with his whole heart. Greg couldn't give that to her and she accepted it. As much as it might kill her, she would move on. For her own sake and her own sanity.

***

The next morning, Emmett swiped his towel over the beautiful wood of Lady Luck.

He turned to Greg. "What do you think?"

Greg wiped a hand across the hardwood cabin. It gleamed in the sunlight. "She looks perfect." Greg turned to Emmett. "You ready to let her go?"

Emmett slowly nodded, unable to tear his gaze from Lady. "I'm ready. And if I'm not, Ashton's on his way to sail her off, so I'd better suck it up. Too late to change my mind now."

Greg squinted. "Does it ever hurt? Working so hard on a boat and knowing you're selling her off to someone else?"

Emmett looked the boat over, arms akimbo, pride gleaming in his eyes. Greg had never seen that look before. Now he knew why Emmett worked so hard. It was for this moment right now, when he could stand tall and look at his work and be proud of what he'd done.

"I enjoy the process," Emmett said. "Once she's fixed up and ready to go, I'm ready for her to go to someone else. I can fix her up, but my days of being out on the water and coming to a close. She deserves someone who'll give her a grand adventure. Someone who'll take care of her. I've got more boats to renovate. To get back in shape. So as long as I know she's going to a good home, I'm fine with it."

Greg nodded.

Emmett winked. "Hope you can buy that boat you've had your eye on."

Greg drew in a breath. "Thanks."

He didn't want to disappoint Emmett right now, although the old guy would find out soon enough that he'd changed his mind about the boat. It had nothing to do with spending the money. He'd lost all desire to sail off on his own.

"You coming back here on your next shore leave?" Emmett asked.

"Not sure yet."

"You let me know when you're coming back so I can be ready for you."

Greg nodded. He looked back at the dock. Emmett's buyer, a man named Ashton Richards, made his way down to the boat, carrying a large duffel bag over his shoulder.

Ashton, all smiles, looked excited about his new purchase and ready to sail away. He and Emmett shook hands.

"She ready for me?" Ashton asked.

"She's ready," Emmett replied.

Ashton nodded. "Good. I plan to be gone within the hour."

"Not wasting any time, eh?"

Ashton's eyes glistened and he grinned. "No."

"I don't blame you. If she were mine I wouldn't waste any time getting her out on the water. Where you headed?" Emmett asked.

"Point Mavery. Off the coast of South Carolina. Got a nice cozy slip waiting for her there. Of course I plan to take her out every chance I get." Ashton turned to Emmett. "I'll take good care of her."

Emmett nodded. "I know you will."

Greg watched Ashton untie the boat, and Emmett followed his every move.

She deserves someone who'll give her a grand adventure. Someone who'll take care of her.

Greg frowned. Melanie deserved that and more, and instead of giving her that, instead of promising her love and a future, he'd been an ass to her. Pretended he didn't care. That he didn't love her. That his heart didn't ache every second without her. How could he have thought about leaving without saying goodbye?

What little joy he'd had in his life had been sucked out of him after she'd left. He'd had joy when he'd been with Melanie. His life felt brighter with her. Being with her was like being home.

Emmett watched the boat take off, and Greg could have sworn he saw tears in his eyes. Now that was a sight Greg never though he'd see. So the old guy wasn't immune to emotion, after all. He might love fixing up boats but letting something he cared about go had to hurt.

Emmett watched the boat disappear and slowly nodded. He pursed his lips. "Lady will be fine with him."

"She will." Greg patted his shoulder. "Ashton will take good care of her."

Emmett nodded. "She'll have adventures. She was made for those."

"Yeah."

After a minute, Emmett let out a deep breath, as if letting go of the sadness he felt having to watch the love of his life move on to better things.

"It's done." Emmett smiled, pulling himself back together. "Back to work, right?"

Greg nodded. "Back to work."

He knew Emmett would be fine. But emptiness filled Greg.

Maybe Emmett could let the love of his life go. He would move on. But Greg couldn't.

Melanie's face flashed before him. The sweetest, best person he'd ever known. She'd stood up for him when no one else in this town had. She'd believed in him when he hadn't believed in himself. She'd brought him out of his pit of despair and self-loathing, and made him want to be a better man. Someone worthy of her. He'd been too blind to see what had been right in front of him, and he'd taken her for granted all this time.

They'd connected in a way he never thought possible. It wasn't just the sex, although sex with her had taken him to another realm. Melanie had taken him to new heights. He'd lost himself when they'd made love.

He hadn't even given her the tender lovemaking she deserved. It had been wild and crazy and abandoned, and he'd received far more pleasure than he'd given her. He wanted to rectify that.

It had been more than sex. He loved her, more than he imagined he'd ever love anyone. He couldn't go the rest of his life without waking up with her in his bed every morning. Coming home to her, spending every minute with her he could. Exploring her, being her shoulder to cry on. He'd be a rock for her, and support her dreams the way she'd support his.

One thing stood in his way. There on the dock, he forgave himself for cheating on Maxine with Erika. He'd done his penance and tortured himself for long enough. What he'd done had been wrong, but it wasn't a mistake he planned to make again.

Maxine had moved on with her life, and so had Erika, and now he needed to move on with his. He let go of the past and looked toward the future. He wanted to be the best person he could for Melanie. He would not screw this up for them.

He needed to find her. Now. He couldn't wait another minute.

"Melanie should have been here by now," he told Emmett. "I thought she'd want to see Lady for the last time."

"She took a day off. Said she's going to check out a college."

"Which one?"

Emmett shrugged. "No clue."

"When was she leaving?"

"This morning, I think."

"Thanks, Emmett. I need the rest of the day off."

Emmett shook a finger at him. "You stay away from that young lady."

Greg just laughed. "If only I could, old friend."

His heart ached for her, and he didn't want to be away from her for another second. The future awaited. A future with her, and he would run after her and find her, no matter what it took.

Chapter Six

Greg stepped hard on the gas, speeding down the two-lane road out of town. He scanned all the cars around him, searching for a beaten-up red Pontiac coupe.

He had no idea where she'd gone, but he planned to check every college and university within a hundred mile radius, asking everyone if they'd seen her. Whatever it took. He felt like a crazy man, but he'd find her.

He smiled when he saw her car broken down on the side of the road near the Route 7 exit. She'd left the hood up and the hazard lights on.

The breakdown had been bad luck on her part, but fate had given him a second chance. And for the first time in his life, he was grateful that the fix-it shop in Wyndham Shores never seemed to actually fix anything right.

Melanie looked so small, standing on the huge expanse of road all alone, and he welcomed the chance to rescue her. She'd rescued him. It was only right that he returned the favor.

Greg pulled his truck in ahead of her car and pulled over. He raced out and ran up to her. "Hey."

She looked up from underneath the hood, surprise in her eyes. "I thought you were long gone by now."

"Not quite."

"Are you on your way out of town?"

He shook his head.

She titled her head. "Where are you headed?"

"To find you. Emmett gave me a lead."

She shook her head. "Don't do this to me, Greg. You made it clear how you felt. Why were you looking for me? To say 'I told you so' about the car?"

"Not hardly," he said softly.

Her dark blue eyes grew hard, but he still saw the softness, the vulnerability underneath. Windows to the soul, indeed. For the first time in his life, Greg saw Melanie. Really saw her.

Her sweet face looked so soft he longed to reach out and touch her. He wanted to kiss her right now, lose himself in the warmth of her sweet lips. He wanted to take her away somewhere they could be alone. Somewhere he could explore every bit of her heart, mind and body. Somewhere he could lose himself inside her, and her in him and it would be the two of them for the rest of their lives. He wanted her for life. Hell, she was the only thing he wanted.

"I'll never tell you I told you so about anything, Mel." He nodded under the hood. "But I would like to help."

She shook her head. "I don't need your help. I've already called Triple A."

She leaned over again and he caught the sight of the smooth skin of her back between her shirt and her jeans. Her jeans fit every curve of her body, and her long brown hair tumbled over her shoulders in waves. Sweet. Hot. Everything he'd dreamed of. She was so beautiful she made his heart stop. Melanie. Beautiful Melanie.

He laughed to himself. He wanted to shout her name a thousand times into the sky, and he'd do it, too, if he didn't fear her thinking he'd lost his mind. Maybe he had lost his mind. He had to have, to have considered leaving her.

He wanted her so much it was all he could do not to take her right here, up against the side of the car. But she deserved better. She deserved a big, comfortable bed where he could pleasure her all night. Every night. If she took him back, he'd spend every day of their lives pleasuring her to the hilt.

"Any idea why the car broke down?" Greg asked.

She shook her head. "They said they'd fixed the problem with the engine. I had the thing in the shop for weeks, but no sooner did I get it out, it stalled on me again."

He reached past her, invading her space. She didn't seem to mind all that much. It felt natural having their bodies so close, and he hoped she felt it, too.

He took a look at the engine, and then underneath the car. It looked like oil leaking out. He stuck the dipstick in and checked her level. It was way too low.

Greg shook his head. "That fixit shop needs to close down. Looks like they changed the oil and didn't put the pan back correctly. You're going to need a tow."

"The truck should be here soon."

He thumbed behind him. "They can tow it to that shop a few miles back. I'll give you a ride wherever you're headed and we can pick it back up on the way home."

"Not necessary. I'll be fine."

She said it so sadly. So firmly. She wanted nothing to do with him and it tore at his heart.

"Mel. I need to talk to you. I'll take you wherever you want to go."

"No." She looked at him with stormy eyes. "You'll be gone soon and I'll have to figure out on my own how to solve my problems. I don't need a ride."

"I'm not getting back in my truck without you in it, Melanie."

"Go on, Greg. I'll figure this out on my own."

"No. I'm not leaving you now. Not ever."

"Don't say things like that.

"Mel, I love you and I don't want to leave you."

She leaned against the car, head down, and folded her arms across her chest. "Right. You've already made it clear how you feel about me, and I've heard every word you said. I get it."

"Just listen to me for a second. I was such an idiot to say those things to you. To pretend like what happened between us meant nothing. I was a coward. An idiot. I didn't want to face how I feel about you, because I figured I'd screw things up between us and you'd hate me in the end. And guess what? My worst fear came true. But I'm not walking away from you."

She slowly raised her head to look at him. Good. Maybe he was getting somewhere.

"You were here all along and I was an idiot not to have noticed. I was always busy with other people and other things, and I didn't see the amazing woman right in front of me."

She bit her lip. "I know. I never told you how I felt about you. I'd hoped you'd figure it out on your own."

"I didn't, and if I hadn't come back here this summer, I still never would have known. But I got the chance to fall in love with you, and I want you in my life. Always."

Melanie blinked away tears.

Greg swept her up in his arms, and it felt so damned good to hold her that he squeezed his eyes shut. "I love you. It's crazy. I've been so miserable for so long, but I'm ready to put it all behind me. I forgive myself for what I did. You're right. I've paid the price. I didn't even see that until you beat me over the head with it. I want to move on. I'm ready."

Greg lifted her chin with the tips of his fingers and looked into her eyes. "You made me see myself in a whole new light. I didn't think I deserved your love. But I want it, and I'm not going to screw it up. I won't let you down. Ever."

She slowly blinked, her eyes filled with pain. "Greg—"

"I see my future with you. I could give you children. We could have as many as you want. I want to give you everything you want and more. I want to support your dreams the way you've always supported me. I will never let anyone hurt you, and I'll do everything in my power to make sure I never hurt you."

Tears slipped from her eyes. "Greg—"

"I pray I'm not too late. Because if I am, I'll spend every second of the rest of my life trying to win you back."

He wanted to wipe away the uncertainty in her eyes. He'd taken her for granted before and he'd never do it again. Ever. He'd cherish her and every second he had with this amazing woman.

"Say yes," he said. If she didn't it would crush his heart and he'd never recover. He needed her to say yes more than he needed to keep breathing. "Say you want to make it work."

After a minute, Melanie gave in and nodded.

Relief like he'd never known filled him. He pulled her against his chest, and his heart burst with need for her. He'd never been so happy.

He'd done it. She was his, and he'd never let her go.

***

That afternoon Greg took Melanie to visit Cillian College on the outskirts of Boston. They toured the campus and the admissions office, grabbing pamphlets and a catalogue of courses. Then they took photos and chatted with some students heading for their summer classes to see how they liked the campus and the courses offered.

Afterward, they had dinner at a tiny little restaurant on the outskirts of the college town.

"What do you think?" Greg asked while they shared a plate of chicken. "Can you see yourself here?"

She nodded.

"We could rent a house off-campus while you're here," he said. "We could call it our home for now. In the meantime we could save up for another place."

"I'd like that." Her brow furrowed and she reached across the table for his hand. "But Greg, with you in the Navy and me in school…would we see each other that much?"

He squeezed her hand. "I'm in this for life, Mel. We'll make it work. We'll be together every second we can. When you finish school I'll get stationed somewhere as close to permanent as I can get. I'll teach and you'll be a nurse. You can work full time, part time…whatever makes you happy. We'll make this work."

She nodded. "Settling down and making a home somewhere sounds good."

"To me, too."

She grinned. "Living by the sea would be good. Doesn't matter which one, but I need to be by the water."

He grinned back at her. "San Diego."

She laughed. "Perfect."

Instead of driving home, they stopped for the night at a B&B halfway between the college and Wyndam Shores.

While she showered, Greg waited for her on the bed. A sense of peace came over him and he felt like a new man. A free man. His heart ached with love for her. No holding back. He knew they belonged together. The two of them together felt more right than anything ever had.

He'd given her his heart and he knew she'd accept him. She'd never throw him away the way he'd been tossed aside before. Love consumed him and he wanted to wrap her up in it and never let her go.

Tonight was all about her, and he intended to pleasure her until she could take no more. Soft and slow. Sweet.

She came out of the bathroom wrapped in a towel, and the sweet look in her eyes as she climbed into bed with him turned him on like nothing ever had. He removed the towel and kissed her breasts. He slowly stroked his tongue over her nipples before drawing one breast into his mouth. He did the same thing to other breast and then kissed her belly, slowly making his way downward. He parted her with his fingers, then sank his tongue between her folds and into her soft flesh as she moaned.

"Greg—"

He licked, kissed, worshipping her sweet body. She tasted like honey and he flicked his tongue over her clit while his fingers sank inside her tight channel. He planned to learn every bit of what she liked. How to draw her close to climax, and how to pull her back and draw out her pleasure as long as he could. He'd learn everything about her, and he'd figure out what gave her the most pleasure. He planned to keep her very happy over the years.

But tonight, right now, Greg needed to be inside her more than he needed to breathe. He sheathed himself in a condom, and when she parted her thighs for him he thought he'd die.

He sank into her slick heat, and she wrapped her legs around him. She was wet for him, and it excited him more than he thought possible. He tried to go slowly, pressing into her an inch at a time, but he needed to be all the way inside her. He thrust deeply and she opened her thighs wider for him, exciting him even more.

He lost himself in the feel of her. He'd never felt this incredible being inside her before. She thrust her hips up to meet him, and he groaned. This was the only place he wanted to be. He drew out his thrusts, wanting to last as long as he could, give her as much pleasure as possible. Give them both as much pleasure as possible.

She reached down and manipulated her clit so that he rubbed against it with each thrust. "Right there," she whispered.

He obliged, wanting to give her an earth-shattering orgasm. Nothing would give him greater pleasure. As he thrust inside her he watched the expressions crossing over her face, trying to figure out how she liked him to move.

Her breathing quickened and she started to turn away as her climax approached.

"Look at me, Mel."

She did, her gaze locked with his as his thrusts became hard. Urgent. Soon he felt the beginning of her tremors. She moaned while her muscles convulsed around him like mini earthquakes against the hard length of him, giving him so much pleasure he had to force himself to hold back his climax so that she could finish.

The hot rush of her release washed over him, exciting him beyond reason. He knew he'd given her an incredible orgasm, and it satisfied something deep in his soul.

He followed shortly afterward with the most intense release of his life. He moved slowly inside her again, drawing out every last ripple of pleasure for both of them.

She gasped for air, her arm thrown over her forehead, eyes closed.

They lay in a tangled heap, sweaty bare limbs entwined, and he knew she'd nearly passed out from pleasure, too.

"Look at me, Melanie."

She blinked her hazy eyes open.

"I love you. I always will." He breathed hard and pressed his lips against her ear.

"I love you, too," she said.

He stroked a damp lock of hair behind her ear. "I don't deserve you, but I want to be worthy of you."

She blinked up at him, still recovering from their intense experience. "You are."

"I'll prove to you every day how much I love you," he said.

Tears streamed down her cheeks. She smiled. "Promise?"

"A promise I intend to give you every day. Marry me, Melanie. Tell me you'll marry me."

"Yes," she said. "I'll marry you, Greg."

Happiness like he'd never known swelled in his heart.

He'd heard the sweetest words he'd ever heard. He held her close, knowing the two of them would last for always. Forever.

About the Author

Anastasia McKellan has always loved losing herself between the pages of a book, and she enjoys writing stories about redemption and love that lasts forever. Her hobbies include taking long walks, studying film history, and hanging out with her two dogs. She currently resides in Washington, D.C. Wherever she is, she'd rather be by the sea. For more on Anastasia, please visit www.chancespress.com.

www.ingramcontent.com/pod-product-compliance
Lightning Source LLC
Chambersburg PA
CBHW071259130626
46556CB00003B/1379